The Sorcerer's Maze Collection

1. The Sorcerer's Maze Adventure Quiz
2. The Sorcerer's Maze Time Machine
3. The Sorcerer's Maze Jungle Trek

Blair Polly & DM Potter

The Sorcerer's Maze Collection

Published by:
The Fairytale Factory,
Wellington,
New Zealand.

YouSayWhichWay.com

ISBN-13: 978-1546367314

ISBN-10: 1546367314

How These Book Works

These are interactive books with YOU as the main character. You will enter the three different sorcerer's mazes and have to find your way out again by answering questions and solving riddles.

You say which way the story goes. Some paths will lead to trouble, others to discovery and adventure. Whichever way you go, you'll be smarter when you get out.

Have fun and follow the link of your choice at the end of each chapter. For example, **P34** means to turn to page 34.

Can you find your way through the sorcerer's mazes? The only way to find out is to get reading!

Oh … and watch out for the sharks, avalanches, and anacondas!

Now for your first decision. Which book would you like to read first?

The Sorcerer's Maze Adventure Quiz? **P1**
The Sorcerer's Maze Time Machine? **P103**
The Sorcerer's Maze Jungle Trek? **P209**

THE SORCERER'S MAZE ADVENTURE QUIZ

(Book One)

1

Enter the maze

Your feet are sinking into a marshmallow floor. You take a few quick steps and find you can stay on top if you keep moving. How did you get here? One moment you were reading and now you are in a long hallway. The place smells of candy and the pink walls are soft when you poke them.

There is a sign hanging from the ceiling that says:

YOU ARE AT THE BEGINNING OF THE SORCERER'S MAZE

But how do you get through to the end of the maze? That is the big question.

Down at the end of the hallway is an old red door. Maybe you should start there?

You take a few bouncy steps, your arms held out to help keep your balance. Getting up would be hard. You don't want to fall.

At last you make it to the red door and try the doorknob.

2

It's locked. You pace in a circle to stop from sinking. When you turn back to the door, you find another sign. On this sign is a question. Below the question are two possible answers. Maybe answering the question correctly will let you open the door.

The questions reads: What is the largest planet in our solar system?

It's time to make your first decision. You may pick right, you may pick wrong, but still the story will go on. What shall it be?

Jupiter? **P4**

Or

Saturn? **P5**

You need to go back to the previous page and make a choice. That is how to get through the maze.

4

You have chosen Jupiter

Jupiter is correct. Jupiter is the fifth planet from the sun and is 88,730 miles in diameter. It takes 11.9 years to orbit the sun.

The lock clicks and the red door opens. You bounce through.

It's dark in the next room with little lights in the ceiling that look like stars, behind you the red door shuts. Where have you ended up? At least you aren't sinking anymore. Instead, you are floating through the air as if there is no gravity. A booming voice begins counting down:

"Ten, nine, eight, seven, six, five, four, three, two, one, blast off!"

Suddenly the room is filled with the roar of rockets. The noise is so loud you have to put your hands over your ears. A streak of light moves across the ceiling, lighting the room and revealing a black door. You push against the wall and float slowly towards it. The new door feels like it's made of metal. Around its edges are rivets. There are some small words stenciled along one edge. The words are another question.

The question reads: Jupiter is the largest planet, but what is the largest mammal on earth?

It is time to make a decision. Which one do you choose?

Blue Whale? **P7**

Or

Elephant? **P8**

You have chosen Saturn

Sorry, that answer is wrong. You can't open the door and go further into the maze. Saturn is only 74,900 miles in diameter, while Jupiter is 88,730.

Did you know that Saturn has rings around it that scientists think are made of ice crystals? Also, did you know that on some dark nights, Saturn is bright enough to see with the naked eye?

Mercury, Venus, Mar, Jupiter and Saturn are all bright enough to see without a telescope, but you have to get away from the city lights. And, if you've got really good eyesight you might just spot Uranus if you know where to look.

If you don't have a telescope, binoculars can help with amateur astronomy too. It's amazing how much more you can see with a little magnification!

But enough facts about Saturn, would you like to try that last question again?

Yes **P2**

Or

No, take me to the correct answer. **P4**

6

Welcome Back to Level 1

There is a sign hanging from the ceiling that says:

OOPS! YOU ARE AT BACK AT THE BEGINNING OF THE SORCERER'S MAZE

Down at the end of the hallway is the same red door.

"Here we go again," you mumble under your breath as you bounce along the squidgy pink floor towards the door.

The door is locked. A sign asks the question you've been asked before.

"At least you should know the answer this time!" a voice booms out, giving you a fright.

The questions reads: What is the largest planet in our solar system?

It is time to make a decision. Which one do you choose?

Jupiter? **P4**

Or

Saturn? **P5**

You have chosen Blue Whale

Well done. Blue Whale is the correct answer. You can open the door.

When you open the door, you just have enough time to take a big breath before you are plunged under the water. As you walk along the seabed, crabs nibble at your toes and starfish crawl across the bottom. Schools of fish swim about, darting from one place to the other like they've all learned the same dance routine.

You try to swim to the surface, but you can't move up. Some strange force is keeping you on the bottom. It must be the sorcerer! But why?

When you look up you see the bottom of a small boat. A rope leads down from the boat to an anchor stuck in the sand not far away. Then you see a shark heading in your direction. And it looks hungry!

You move over to the rope, thinking you can use it to pull yourself up to the surface but there is a note attached to the rope. It says: You must answer this question quickly or you will get eaten. If you answer it correctly, you can come to the surface. The question reads: There are approximately 2000 species of starfish, but are they really fish?

It is time to make a quick decision. Which one do you choose?

Yes, starfish are a strange type of fish. **P10**

Or

No, starfish aren't fish at all. **P11**

8

You have chosen Elephant

I'm sorry elephant, is incorrect. Did you know that there are two different types of elephant? There are Asian elephants and African elephants.

"But what is the difference?" you say.

Well for a start African elephants (like the one in the picture) are much heavier, they have bigger ears, bigger tusks, and their skin is more wrinkled.

African elephants eat mainly leaves, while Asian elephants eat mainly grass.

So how much do you think an African elephant weighs?

It's time to make a choice, but be careful. If you chose wrong you'll end up back at the start. There is a hint in the information above, so which answer do you think is more likely to be correct?

An African elephant weighs 4000 to 7000kg **P9**

Or

An African elephant weights 3000 to 6000kg **P6**

An African elephant weighs 4000 to 7000 kg

What a great answer. You picked the heavier of the two choices. Good skills. This means you'll be able to move on through the maze.

An African elephant weighs 4000 to 7000 kilograms. That's 8,800 to 15,400 pounds. But a blue whale is much bigger. They can weigh 200 tons, (that's 400,000 pounds or a little over 181,000 kg). That's as much as 25 elephants!

It is time to make a decision. Which one of these is bigger?

An elephant? **P8**

Or

A blue whale? **P7**

10

You have chosen yes, that starfish are a type of fish

Wow, funny looking fish. Where are its fins or gills? Even though they are called starfish (or sea stars), they aren't actually fish at all. They are echinoderms. They got the name starfish because of their shape. Starfish come in all sorts of colors.

Starfish like to eat mussels, clams and other shell fish. Their mouth is on the underside of their body. Some starfish can weigh over 10 pounds!

Now that you know more about starfish, let's go back and try that last question once again.

Go back **P7**

You have chosen NO, starfish aren't fish

You have answered correctly and can pull yourself up the rope. But hurry the shark is right behind you.

When you reach the surface, a boy about your age helps you climb aboard. The boat is small and doesn't have a motor. There are two oars lying in the bottom and a small net with a couple of silver fish caught in its mesh.

"Thanks for helping me," you tell the boy.

The shark is circling the boat but the boy is very relaxed about it so you act casual too.

When you look around, all you can see is water. "How far from land are we?"

"I'm not exactly sure," the boy says. "But I'm sure we could work it out."

"How will we do that?" you ask.

"Well let's see. When I started rowing, I left the beach and went west for 21 miles. Then I turned north and rowed another 6 miles. Then I rowed east for 9 miles. Then south for 4 miles, then east again for 3 miles then south for 2 miles. Then west again for 6 miles.

The boy looks at you and says, "If you answer this correctly I'll row you to shore."

You think hard, trying to work out the answer to the boy's question. "But why are you here?" you ask.

The boy smiles. "Because I'm the sorcerer's apprentice. I'm here to help."

That makes sense. You are in the sorcerer's maze after all.

12

"Hey, it's time to make a decision," the boy says. "Are we 14 or 15 miles from shore?

Which one do you choose?"

Is it 14 miles to shore? **P13**

Or

Is it 15 miles to shore? **P16**

You have decided that it's 14 miles to shore

Unfortunately that is wrong. The correct answer is 15. It's a shame that you didn't get this correct because now you have three more problems to do before you can open the next part of the story.

7 x 8 =

4 x 11 =

5 x 20 =

It is time to make a decision. Which three numbers below are correct?

64, 44 and 90? **P15**

Or

56, 44 and 100? **P14**

14

You have chosen 56, 44 and 100

That's better. You got it right this time. You can move on to Level Two.

Go to Level Two **P22**

You have chosen 64, 44 and 90

Oops, that's not right. Maybe you rushed it. You can use a calculator if you want to.

What would you like to do?

Go back and have another go? **P13**

Or

Go back to the beginning of the maze? **P1**

16

You have decided that it's 15 miles to shore

"That was a tough one. I didn't think you'd get it right," the boy says. "I suppose I'd better get rowing."

He puts the oars into the rowlocks and moves to the bench seat. The shark stops circling and starts bashing the underside of the boat. You hold onto the sides and try to keep it stable.

"Hurry!" you say.

The boy takes the oars, dips them into the water, and pulls hard. He is remarkably strong. The little boat glides across the water as fast as a boat with a motor. Soon, the shark is left far behind.

"That was a white pointer by the way," the boy says. "One of the most vicious predators of the sea."

"So that's why you're rowing so fast," you say with a grin.

"A shark could never eat me. I'm the sorcerer's apprentice. I'd just turn him into a tuna and have him for lunch." He points to the fish in the bottom of the boat, "... like those ones."

An hour later, through the mist and haze, you see land in the distance.

"How do you know which way to go?" you ask the boy.

He reaches into his pocket and pulls out a compass. "This tells me all I need to know. But if you can tell me how many degrees there are on my compass dial you can go straight to level 2 of the maze."

17

But what is the answer to his question? How many degrees are there on a compass? Isn't it the same number as the degrees in a circle?

It is time for you to choose.

Are there 260 degrees on a compass? **P18**

Or

Are there 360 degrees on a compass? **P22**

18

You have chosen that there are 260 degrees on a compass

"Just as well I'm doing the navigation," the boy says. "There are 360 degrees on my compass, see?"

You squint at the tiny numbers on the dial.

"The four main directions on a compass are north, east, south, and west. Each quadrant has 90 degrees. And, as we all know 4 x 90 is 360."

"How did you work that out so fast?" you ask the boy.

The boy smiles. "Easy, I multiplied 4 x 9 and then added the 0 back on again. 4 x 9 = 36. Add the zero back on and you get 360."

"Wow that's a cool trick," you say. "Does it work with other numbers?"

"Let's try it," the boy says. "You do 6 x 40."

"Okay," you say. "6 times 4 is 24, add the zero and I get 240."

"Correct!" the boy says. "There's all sort of tricks to learn when it comes to making math easy."

The boy stops rowing. "My arms are getting tired. I'll give

19

you one more chance, and if you get it right you can go straight to LEVEL 2 of the maze."

"Sounds good to me," you say.

He scratches his head. "Okay, try this one. What is 9 x 30?"

You're keen to go straight to LEVEL 2 so you use the trick you've just learned.

Is it:

270? **P22**

Or

180? **P20**

20

You have chosen 180

"Oops, you got that one wrong," the boy says. "Remember how the trick goes?"

"Umm … I must have forgotten," you mumble.

"Let's try it again," the boy says. "9 x 3 is 27. Then add the 0 back on to the end and the correct answer is 270."

"Oh yeah, I've got it now," you say.

Over the boys shoulder, you notice a boat-sized speck getting rapidly larger. "Hey there's a freighter steaming right towards us," you tell the boy. "I can see containers stacked on board."

"Freighter? I don't see a freighter."

"Turn around!" you yell. "The boat is getting closer really fast. It's going to run us over if you don't move us out of the way!"

The boy just grins. "Well you'd better answer this question correctly then. Otherwise we'll sink and you'll have to go all the way back to the beginning of the maze."

"All the way back?" you ask. "That's unfair."

"Who said anything about the sorcerer is fair? He's full of tricks to trip you up. So think hard and choose wisely."

Meanwhile, the freighter has gone from the size of a house to the size of a … freighter!

"Hurry up," you say. "It's nearly here."

The boy reaches into his bag and pulls out a rock and an apple.

"Right," he says. "Which weighs more, a pound of apples

or a pound of rocks?"

Quick! It's time to make a decision. Which one of these three answers is correct?

A pound of apples weighs more. **P6**

Or

A pound of rocks weighs more. **P1**

Or

They both weigh the same. **P22**

22

Welcome to Level Two

A seething mass of ants on the forest floor in front of you have formed themselves into a message. It says: Welcome to Level 2.

You walk around the ants and along a path. Up ahead is a fork in the trail. Standing in the middle of the fork is the sorcerer's apprentice.

"How did I get here?" you ask.

The boy gives you a cheeky smile. "It's the sorcerer. He'll dump you anywhere to keep you from finding a way out of his maze."

"You mean I'll never get out?"

"Oh, you'll get out eventually," the boy says. "It just depends on how good you are at answering questions and solving riddles."

"And if I'm not very good?" you ask.

The boy pulls an energy bar out of his pocket and holds it out towards you. "Here, you might need this for later."

You slip it into your pocket thinking it was good you had

a big breakfast. "What now?"

The boy reaches into his other pocket and pulls out a piece of paper. "This is a question the sorcerer gave me earlier. Good luck."

You suspect you may need it.

The boy holds the note up so he can read it in the dim light filtering through the tree branches. "Okay, here goes. Mount Everest is the world's highest mountain, on the border of Nepal and Tibet. What year was it climbed for the very first time?"

It is time to make a choice. Which is correct?

Mt. Everest was first climbed by Edmund Hillary and Tenzing Norgay in 1993. **P24**

Or

Mt. Everest was first climbed by Edmund Hillary and Tenzing Norgay in 1953. **P26**

24

You've chosen that Mt. Everest was first climbed in 1993

"You were only 40 years out," the sorcerer's apprentice says. "The correct answer is 1953."

"40 years is way out." you say. "But how was I meant to know that?"

The boy shrugs. "I don't know. Take it up with the sorcerer next time you see him."

"What can you tell me then? Can you tell me how to get out of this forest?" you ask.

"Maybe you can hitch a ride on a bear."

"A bear?" You look around nervously.

"What about a wolf?" the boy teases. "Or maybe an eagle could give you a lift?"

Has the boy gone mad? Why is he talking of wild animals? You half expect these wild animals to appear at any moment. "The sorcerer wouldn't put me in danger would he?" you ask.

"You never know with the sorcerer," the boy says. "Okay it's time for your next question."

You don't want to get this next one wrong so you listen carefully.

"Okay," the boy says. "On which continent would you find bears, wolves and eagles?"

North America? **P37**

Or

Africa? **P35**

Welcome back to Level Two

A seething mass of ants on the forest floor in front of you have formed a message. It says:

WELCOME BACK TO LEVEL TWO

You walk around them and along path. Up ahead is a fork in the trail. Standing in the middle of the path is the sorcerer's apprentice.

"How did I end up here again?" you ask.

The boy gives you a cheeky smile. "When you answer wrong, the sorcerer will dump you anywhere to keep you from finding a way out of his maze."

"How long will it take me to get out?"

"It depends on you," the boy says. "At least you should know this next question. After all you've answered it before."

The boy holds the note up so he can read it in the dim light coming through the tree branches. "Okay, here goes … again. Mount Everest is the world's highest mountain on the border of Nepal and Tibet. What year was it climbed for the very first time?"

It is time to make a choice. Which is correct?

Mt. Everest was first climbed by Edmund Hillary and Tenzing Norgay in 1993. **P24**

Or

Mt Everest was first climbed by Edmund Hillary and Tenzing Norgay in 1953. **P26**

26

You've chosen that Mt. Everest was first climbed in 1953

"Wow what a good answer," the boy says through a scarf wrapped around his face. "1993 wasn't all that long ago so 1953 was far more likely to be right. Did you know that Edmund Hillary was a beekeeper from New Zealand?"

You pull up the hood of your parka up and shake your head.

"And Tenzing Norgay was a Sherpa guide from Nepal. They were part of a British expedition that first conquered the mountain in May of 1953."

"Interesting," you say. "But we're standing on top of a mountain and it's freezing!"

Why has the sorcerer dumped you way up here? It's just as well he's given you some warm clothing otherwise you'd turn into a block of ice.

The sorcerer's apprentice is laughing. "Quite a view from the top of the world, eh?"

"It certainly is," you say, looking out over the Himalayas. "Hey, how are we breathing up here?"

"The air is thin up here, but we can last a couple of minutes. Imagine what it must have been like to stand here for the very first time," the boy says. "It must have been quite an experience."

There are snow-covered mountains in every direction. The wind is blowing and your nose has an icicle hanging from it. "It's quite an experience right now!" you say, stomping your feet to stay warm. "How are we meant to get down?"

The sorcerer's apprentice pulls up his collar and looks towards a nasty-looking bank of clouds heading in your direction. "Well, we could climb down, but that might take some time. Besides it looks like an ice storm is on its way. We don't want to climb through that!"

You look towards the clouds. "If I solve a riddle, will you get me off this mountain?"

The sorcerer's apprentice reaches into his down-filled jacket. "It just so happens I've got one of those handy."

The piece of paper is very small so hopefully the riddle won't be too difficult.

"Okay, here we go," the boy says. "What stays in a corner, while traveling to Nepal?"

You scratch your head. "Umm … that's a sticky one."

The boy looks at you and shivers. "Quick before we freeze. Which of these five answers is correct?"

1. A suitcase **P1**
2. A box **P6**
3. A stamp **P28**
4. An airline pilot **P30**
5. A mountain climber **P6**

28

You have chosen stamp

"Well done. That is correct. You can move on through the sorcerer's maze," the sorcerer's apprentice says.

A buzz fills the air and you start to spin around, faster and faster.

"Hang on!" the boy yells. "We're being sucked into one of the sorcerer's vortexes."

Things go black for a moment, then the spinning begins to slow.

When the movement stops, you find yourself in a room filled with letters, packages, conveyor belts and people sorting bags of mail.

"Did you know that over 19 billion postage stamps were printed in the United States in 2014?" the boy asks.

"Really, that many?"

"Did you know that the very first stamp was called a Penny Black, and it was issued in the United Kingdom in May 1840?"

"No," you say.

"Nowadays lots of people collect stamps. Some like to save stamps from a particular country. Others choose a theme like transportation or flowers. Some just collect everything from anywhere."

"They must really love stamps," you say. "But what now? Am I getting near the end of the maze?"

"You've still got a bit more maze to get through. Would you like another question?"

"Sure. After that can we go to lunch?"

The boy nods. "Sure. Do you like pizza?"

"Is that my question? Because that's an easy one!" you say, grinning.

"No that one doesn't count. But how about this. Where did pizza originate?"

It is time to make a decision. Which is correct?

Pizza came from Italy. **P43**

Or

Pizza was invented in the United States. **P39**

30

Oops. The right answer is stamp

An envelope suddenly appears in the boy's hand.

"That just appeared out of thin air," you say. "What the heck's going on?"

The boy looks as shocked as you are. "I don't know. But speaking of thin air, did you know that the air up this high has 66% less oxygen in it than it does at sea level?"

"Great! So we're going to suffocate *and* freeze?"

"Nah," the boy says. "I've got some questions in my pocket. Why don't you try one of those?"

"Read it quickly, I'm freezing."

The sorcerer's apprentice pulls out another piece of paper. "Okay this should be easy. What nationality were the first people to climb Mt. Everest without bottled oxygen?"

It is time to make a decision. Were they:

Vulcan and Martian? **P31**

Or

Austrian and Italian? **P33**

You have chosen Vulcan and Martian

"Mr. Spock, from *Star Trek*, was Vulcan," the sorcerer's apprentice says. "He was the one with the pointy ears. But he's only a fictional character, not a real person."

"Oh that's right," you say.

"And, as far as we know, there's no such thing as men from Mars, apart from in science fiction, so I doubt they'll be climbing the world's highest peak anytime soon."

Then suddenly you feel yourself spinning at great speed. Colors fly around you head like a million butterflies. Everything goes quiet.

Things go dark and you can't see the sorcerer's apprentice. You can't even see your hand in front of your face. Somewhere in the distance, water drips. *Plonk, plonk, plonk.*

"Where am I?" you say into the darkness, not really sure if you'll get an answer or not.

"You are in my cave!" booms a loud voice.

"Who are you?" you ask, afraid of what the answer might be.

"I am the sorcerer!"

"Why am I in the dark?"

Footsteps walk towards you. "Because I don't let anyone see me until they get to the end of the maze."

"Why?"

"Because that's how I want it!" the voice booms.

What's all the mystery about? "How do I get to the end of

the maze?"

"You can start by answering this next question. If you get the answer right, I have a surprise for you. But if you get it wrong you'll have to go all the way back to the very beginning of the maze."

"All the way back?" you say. "That doesn't seem fair."

"Ah but it's a simple question. You should have no problem," the sorcerer says.

You hope he's right. But for some reason, you don't really trust him.

"The question is," the sorcerer says. "How long is a piece of string?"

"What sort of question is that?" you say. "That's silly!"

"Ha ha ha!" the sorcerer laughs. "That is the correct answer."

"Phew!" you say.

"It is time to make a decision," the voice booms. "Which would you like?"

A surprise? **P41**

Or

Pizza? **P43**

You have chosen Italian and Australian

"Correct! But then you probably know that men from Mars are just fiction, so it's pretty unlikely they'd be doing much mountain climbing!"

"True," you say.

"The first two mountaineers to climb Mt. Everest without bottled oxygen were Peter Habeler from Austria, and Reinhold Messner from Italy."

"Those two must have had pretty good lungs," you say.

"That's right. Because the amount of oxygen in the air becomes less the higher you climb, most mountain climbers start using bottled oxygen at 26,000 feet. Mt. Everest is just over 29,000 feet, so climbing Everest without extra oxygen made a difficult climb even harder."

"They must be nuts," you say. "So where's this lunch you promised?"

With a bright flash and a puff of smoke you are taken off the mountain.

You find yourself in a large room full of people. The sorcerer's apprentice is standing beside you. "I smell pizza!" he says.

You can smell it too. It smells delicious. "I'm hungry. Can we get some?"

The sorcerer's apprentice nods. "Sure we can. But only if you answer this next question correctly."

You feel your stomach rumbling and cross your fingers hoping for an easy one.

"Where did pizza come from?" the boy asks.
It is time for you to choose.
What do you say?
Pizza came from Italy. **P43**
Or
Pizza was invented in the United States. **P39**

You have chosen Africa

"Unfortunately Africa isn't right," the boy says. "Africa has an eagle called the fish eagle, and one wolf species that lives in Eritrea and parts of Ethiopia, but it doesn't have bears anymore."

"What happened to the bears?" you ask.

"There was a bear that lived in the Atlas Mountains of Libya and Morocco, but it is now believed to be extinct."

"How do you know this stuff?" you ask the boy. "Is it because you're the sorcerer's apprentice?"

"No it's because I was stuck in the maze for three weeks and learned lots of things."

"Three weeks? I hope it doesn't take me that long to get out."

The boy laughs. "It won't. I was only five when I first arrived. You're older so you should get through much quicker."

"Phew! You had me worried there."

"But you will need to be clever and work hard to get out," the boys says.

"Well let's do it!" you say.

"Right. This part is a bit different," the boy says. "If you get it right, we go to lunch and have pizza."

"Different? How?"

"Imagine you are standing on a big X looking straight ahead."

"Yeah, okay."

36

"Now concentrate. Turn to your right. Then turn to your right again. Then turn right once more. Now, turn left. And then turn left again. Now turn right, and right again, and right one last time."

"Okay. I think I've got it."

"It is time to answer a question. If you answer correctly you can go have pizza. If not you're in for a big surprise."

It is time to make a decision. Pick one of these two statements.

I am looking in the opposite direction to where I started. **P41**

Or

I am looking in the same direction that I started in. **P43**

You have chosen North America

"Well done," the boy says. "North America is correct."

"I'm glad of that," you say.

"In North America there are three types of bear. Grizzly bears, which are also called brown bears. Then there are black bears. And finally, in parts of Canada and Alaska, polar bears. Did you know that black bears aren't always black?

"Really?"

The boy nods. "They can also be various shades of brown, black or even white. They estimate the black bear population to be somewhere in the region of 900,000."

"Wow, that's a lot of bears," you say.

"There aren't so many polar bears though," he says. "Only 22,000 or so."

"That still seems a lot."

"Yeah, but that covers a big area. They live way up north in the arctic. Which makes me think of a question."

"Another one?"

"If you want to get through the maze, you need to get them right."

"But I'm hungry," you say to the boy.

"Okay, if you get this one right, we can go have pizza."

Your stomach growls like a grizzly bear. "Deal."

"Here's your question. In which country do most of the world's polar bears live?"

You scratch your head.

"Think hard because if you miss this one, the sorcerer told me I have to send you back to the beginning of Level one."

"But that's all the way back to the beginning!"

"I know. Remember though, if you get this one right you

38

get pizza!"

It is time to make your choice.

Do most of the world's polar bears live in:

Canada **P43**

Or

The United States **P6**

Pizza was invented in the United States

Sorry, but that answer is incorrect.

The term 'pizza' came from Naples, Italy, back in the 16th century.

However, many cultures ate similar foods well before then. In fact archeologists have found evidence of bread making in Sardinia from more than 7,000 years ago, although the flat breads they made back then would have little resemblance to the cheesy slabs served up in pizza restaurants around the globe today.

"Why did you choose the United States?" the boy says. "Now we'll never get any pizza."

"Hey, you're the sorcerer's apprentice," you say. "Surely you have more questions you can ask me?"

The boy digs deep in his pockets and comes up empty. "No questions, I'm afraid."

Your stomach rumbles. "What's that paper sticking out of your top pocket then?" you ask, pointing.

"Oh, that's not a question. That's a riddle. Would you like one of those instead?"

You nod. "Yes please."

He pulls out the paper and reads: "Billy's mother has five children. Susan, Mary, Thomas and Jack are the names of four of them. What is the fifth child's name?"

It is time to make a decision.

Which of these five answers is right?

Answer this correctly and you can go have pizza for

40

lunch. If not you're in for a surprise.

1. Mary **P41**
2. Jack **P22**
3. Susan **P6**
4. Billy **P43**
5. Thomas **P1**

Surprise!

Well, I bet you didn't think you'd end up in a long pink hallway that smells of candy. Sound familiar?

But don't worry, you haven't been sent back to the beginning of the maze. You're in a candy land with marshmallow walls and bowls of chocolates and caramels just waiting to be eaten.

The sorcerer's apprentice is sitting in a big overstuffed chair at the far end of the hallway with a big box of chocolates in his lap. "So you found my little secret, eh?" the boy says.

You look around in wonder as you walk towards him. Never before have you seen so many sugary sweets in one place. "But what about your teeth? Won't they fall out if you eat all this?"

The boy opens his mouth to reveal black stumps and swollen gums. "What teeth?" he says.

"Ewww!" you say, smelling his bad breath, even though he's still yards away. "That's horrible."

Then you notice the boy has grown claws where his fingers once were. In a flash, his shirt turns into green scales and a forked tongue shoots out of his mouth.

"Come closer," the creature says. "You look tasty!"

"You're not the sorcerer's apprentice! You're a lizard monster!" you say drawing back. "What have you done with my friend?"

The thing burps. "I'm so sick of candy, I ate him for

42

lunch."

You're in trouble. You turn and run towards a door at the other end of the hallway. On the door is a piece of paper with a picture and a question on it.

To open the door, you'll need to answer the question.

What animal is this?

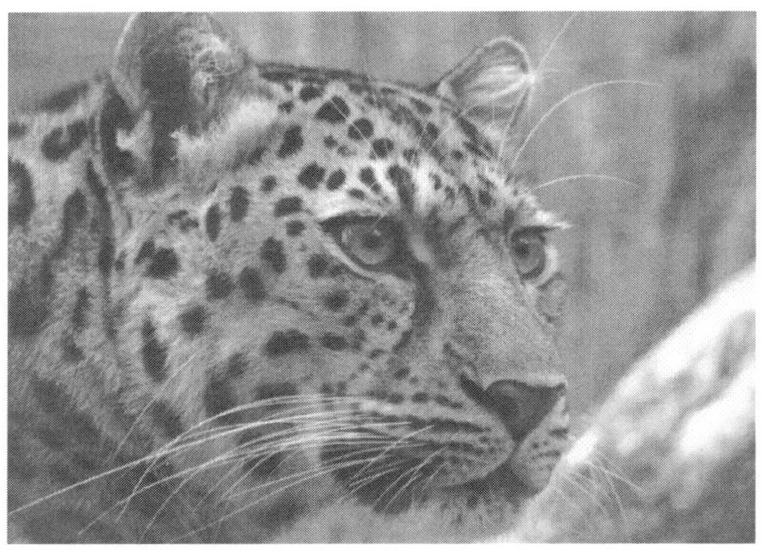

Make a quick decision. Hurry!

Is this big cat:

A tiger? **P45**

Or

A leopard? **P46**

Yippee, you get to have some pizza!

The smell of pizza is everywhere. But maybe you don't like pizza? Maybe you'd like ice cream or fruit instead?

"In the sorcerer's pizza parlor you can have almost anything you want. All you have to do is answer a question or two," the sorcerer's apprentice says, reading your mind.

"Pizza is fine," you say.

You join the sorcerer's apprentice where he is sitting behind a long table with a group of others.

"I'd like to introduce you to my friends," he says. "This is Billy, Jack, Susan, Mary and Thomas."

The kids all have a similar look. "Are you related?"

Jack answers. "How did you guess? Do we look that similar?"

They not only look similar, Susan and Mary are twins.

"Yes you do," you say, taking a seat.

"Before you eat," the sorcerer's apprentice says, "you've just got one more question to answer. But if you get it wrong. You'll have to go all the way back to the beginning of Level 2."

"Aww!" you cry out. "I want pizza."

"But wait!" the sorcerer's apprentice says. "If you get it right, you get to jump all the way to the end of Lever 2. Isn't that good?"

You're so hungry you just want to get it over with. "Okay what's the question?"

"Okay here it is." The boy pulls a picture out of his

44

pocket and lays it on the table. "What animal is this?"

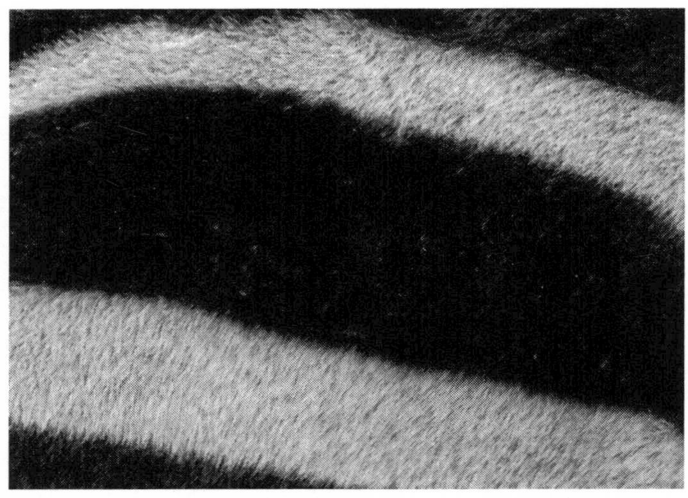

It is time to make a decision.

Which of these three animals is correct?

1. tiger **P45**
2. panda **P41**
3. zebra **P51**

You have chosen tiger

"Aw well, better luck next time. A leopard has spots and a tiger has stripes. At least you'll know the correct answer next time. Let's try another animal question," the sorcerer's apprentice says. "I bet you'll get this one."

"Okay," you say. "But if I get it right, can I go to Level 3?"

The boy nods. "Sure, but with reward comes risk. I'll let you go to the end of Level 3 if you get this right, but if you get it wrong…"

"I have to go back to the beginning?"

"Correct," the sorcerer's apprentice says.

"Okay," you say. "I'll take the chance."

"Really? Without knowing what the question is?" the boy says.

You nod. "I just want to get to the end so I can eat."

"Okay. You asked for it." He pulls a piece of paper out of his pocket and shows it to you.

The question reads: If you mix blue and yellow together what color do you get?

It is time to make a choice. Is it:

Purple? **P25**

Or

Green? **P51**

You have chosen leopard

"Well done!" a voice booms. "That is correct. You can open the door and escape the lizard monster."

You stumble through and hear a reassuring click behind you. There is a thud as the monster hits the now closed door. "Phew that was close!"

"Yes it was!" booms the voice.

You are in a rectangular box. It smells like plywood and sawdust. Light filters down through air holes cut in the top. Wood shavings litter the box's bottom.

The walls are smooth and you can see writing on one of them.

The writing says:

TO GET OUT OF THIS BOX YOU'LL NEED TO ANSWER A TRICK QUESTION.

"Not more questions!" you say in frustration.

In a puff of smoke, the sorcerer's apprentice arrives. "I hear the sorcerer had to help you on that last one."

You nod. "Saved me in the nick of time."

"He's good like that. Now don't get fooled on this next question," he says. "Think very, very carefully. This is a really tricky question."

"Is it?" you ask, wondering what you're in for.

The sorcerer's apprentice nods. He looks serious.

"Now think carefully," he says. "How many walls does this box we're in have?"

Walls? Why do they need to know that? you wonder.
It is time to make a choice. Which is correct?
The box has 6 walls. **P48**
Or
The box has 4 walls. **P50**

You have chosen that the box has 6 walls

"Oops. That was a slip up," the sorcerer's apprentice says. "Remember how the air holes were cut into the 'top' of the box and the wood shavings were on the 'bottom'?"

"Yeah but…"

"So the box has a top, a bottom and 4 walls. The tricky part of the question was when I tried to make you think the question was hard, when it was really quite simple."

"That's a bit unfair," you say.

The boy shrugs. "It was a trick. That's what sorcerers do. Don't worry. You've got a chance to reach the end of Level 2 with this next question. But beware, if you get this wrong you'll have to go all the way back to the very beginning of the maze."

The boy pulls a bag out of one pocket. From the other he pulls out 12 marbles. "Right now concentrate."

The boy opens the top of the bag and drops in two marbles. Then he drops in two more. Then he drops in three marbles. Then four more. Then he takes out three, then puts two more back in. Then he takes five marble out of the bag. So how many marbles are left in his hand?

It is time to make your decision. Which is correct?

There are 5 marbles. **P49**

Or

There are 7 marbles. **P51**

Oh no, you've gone all the way back to Level 1

You find yourself back in a long hallway. The place smells of candy and has pink walls that feel like marshmallow when you poke them. The floor is bounces as you walk around. When you don't move you sink.

There's that sign again. It says:

YOU ARE ENTERING THE SORCERER'S MAZE … AGAIN!

Down at the end of the hallway is a familiar looking red door. You are beginning to hate this door.

You take a few bouncy steps and give it a kick. Then you try the knob. It is locked of course. Beside the door is the same old sign.

The question still reads: What is the largest planet in our solar system?

The sorcerer's apprentice appears. "I'll give you a hint," he says. "The answer hasn't changed!"

So, which one do you choose?

Jupiter? **P4**

Or

Saturn? **P5**

50

You have chosen that that box has 4 walls

"Well done," the boy says. "Yes the box has 4 walls, a top and a bottom. Were you tempted to pick 6?"

"I was for a moment," you confess.

"The tricky part of the question was that I tried to make you think that the question was tricky when it was really pretty simple."

In a puff of smoke you find yourself sitting in an empty room tied to a chair. The floors are wooden and the walls are white. It looks like an art gallery, but there aren't any pictures on the walls. How did you end up here? It must be that pesky sorcerer again.

There is no sign of the boy. No sounds. No smells. No sharks. No ants.

Twisting your neck as far as it goes, you see a poster on the wall to your left. The printing on the poster is small, but you can just make it out. It is another one of those infernal questions!

The poster reads: You can move on to the end of Level 2 if you get this correct. If you get it wrong you will have to go back to the beginning of this level. Think carefully and pick the correct answer.

The question reads: The blood pumping around your body is called your:

Rotation? **P25**

Or

Circulation? **P51**

Welcome to Level 3

If this is your first time at Level 3, congratulations.

If you've been here before, you'll have to work your way through this level again. But look on the bright side. You're older and wiser this time.

"Well here you are," the sorcerer's apprentice says. "Level three is quite tricky."

"But why are we in the jungle?" you ask looking around at the dense foliage.

The boy acts as if he's just noticed. "That's a very good question."

You expect him to say more, but he doesn't. He just stands there looking at you.

"Well," you say. "Do you know why we're here or not?"

The boy grins. "You're not very observant are you?"

You look around again, trying to spot what the boy is alluding to. But all you see is jungle, with towering trees, ferns, and broad-leafed plants.

"What am I missing?" you ask.

The boy pretends he doesn't hear you and stares above your head.

You look up just in time to see that a huge boa constrictor hanging from a branch above you is about to wrap itself around your neck. You jump back.

"Whoa! Look at the size of that!"

But the boy isn't listening. He is staring off into space his head bent listening to….

"I hear water!" you say. "Should we head towards it?"

The boy speeds off down a narrow path. "Race you there!" he calls over his shoulder.

You take off after him. "Hey, wait up!"

After running for a few minutes, you feel a fine mist against your face. The sound of the water is getting louder. As you come into a clearing you see a towering waterfall.

"Wow," you pant as you look up and up and up. "This is amazing. It just keeps going!"

"It's called Angel Falls. It's the tallest in the world," the sorcerer's apprentice shouts over the roar of water. "Fifteen times taller than Niagara Falls."

You're not surprised it's the highest. The cliff rises vertically for thousands of feet. Little rainbows form in the mist where the sunlight hits it.

"So why are we here?" you ask.

The boy reaches for a piece of paper in his pocket. "It probably has to do with the sorcerer's next question."

Somehow you suspected this was coming.

"Okay, here we go," the boys says. "What country are we in?"

It is time to make a decision if you are to move on through the maze. Is the correct answer:

Brazil? **P53**

Or

Venezuela? **P63**

You have chosen Brazil

Unfortunately, Brazil is not the right answer. Although Brazil borders Venezuela, Angel Falls is well north of the Brazilian border in Venezuela. The falls were given their European name after pilot, Jimmy Angel, who discovered them in 1933 while searching for ore.

Venezuela may have the highest waterfall, but did you know that Brazil is the largest country in South America with a land area of over 5 million square miles? Brazil is the fifth largest country on earth behind Russia, Canada, China and the United States.

"So you chose Brazil, eh?" the sorcerer's apprentice says. "Do you know what that means?"

"No," you answer. "What?"

"It means we have to paddle."

All of a sudden you find yourself in a dugout canoe in the middle of a river. You have a paddle in your hand and the sorcerer's apprentice sits in the narrow boat in front of you.

The river is incredibly wide, the water a murky brown. A huge ship passes, heading upriver half a mile away.

"Where are we?" you ask the boy. "I've never seen a river so wide."

"We're still in Brazil," the boy says. "This is the biggest river in South America. But do you know its name?"

"Maybe," you say. "Are you going to give me a couple choices?"

"Yeah sure," he says. "I'll give you a list of three."

54

It is time for you to make a decision.

What is the name of South America's biggest river?

1. Nile **P60**
2. Congo **P41**
3. Amazon **P55**

You have chosen the Amazon

Well done. The Amazon is correct. The Amazon is the second longest river in the world, only the Nile in Africa is longer. However, the Amazon does carry a larger volume of water than the Nile. It runs all the way across Brazil and into Peru.

The boy starts paddling towards shore. "Did you know that the Amazon rainforest has more animal species than anywhere else on earth? More than one third of all the animals live here, and over 3000 species of fish!"

"Doesn't the world's largest snake live here too?" you ask.

"That's right, the anaconda. It's a water snake, so I'd keep paddling if I were you."

You see birds sitting in the trees lining the shore. There are splashes in the river around you. "It's probably got the most insects too!" you say, swatting at a mosquito that's landed on your arm. "Got any bug spray?"

The boy rustles in his pockets and pulls out a tube of insect repellent while the canoe rocks back and forth. "Here, try some of this; the mosquitoes around here carry all sorts of diseases. Yellow fever, malaria, dengue fever, and more. Did you know more people get killed by mosquitoes every year than all the snakes and lions and wolves, alligators and spiders put together?"

"Really?" you say, quick to get the top off the tube and spread the cream on your arms, neck, and face. "So why did the sorcerer put us here?"

56

"Oh, he has his reasons. When we get to shore I'll tell you."

You pass the repellent back to the boy. Then grabbing your paddle you follow the boy's lead and make long strokes through the water. Ten minutes later, you and the boy are pulling the dugout up onto the bank of the river.

"Come this way," the boy says, heading off into the jungle. "I want to show you something."

The jungle is thick. And there are strange noises everywhere. High up in the canopy, a group of monkeys with thin arms and legs and long tails leap about gathering food and going about their lives. They are very agile and move around the treetops with ease.

"Would you like a question?" the sorcerer's apprentice asks. "You do want to finish the maze don't you?"

"Okay," you say, but actually this is a pretty cool place and you're enjoying the visit.

The boy nods and pulls a piece of paper out of his pocket. "Which of the following is a type of monkey?"

It is time to make a decision. Which of these five do you choose?

1. bird monkey **P59**
2. alligator monkey **P41**
3. scorpion monkey **P59**
4. spider monkey **P57**
5. lizard monkey **P6**

You have chosen spider monkey

"Well done," the sorcerer's apprentice says. "Those are definitely spider monkeys up there. Now all you have to do is answer one more question and you've made it to Level 4. Isn't that exciting?"

"I did like the jungle though," you say, looking at your new surroundings. "What's with all this sand?"

The sorcerer's apprentice looks around. "Hmmm … this is weird."

"You mean you don't know where we are?"

"Oh I know. We're in the Sahara Desert. It's just that I could have sworn I parked my camel here."

"Your camel?"

"Well you don't want to walk 300 miles in this heat do you?"

You turn and look around. For as far as you can see, all you see is sand. "300 miles? Are you serious?"

"I told you the sorcerer was tricky. He wants you to stay a while longer, so he's making it difficult for you."

"But what did I do to him?"

"That's not the point. You're making it through his maze too quickly and he doesn't like that. He prides himself on making hard mazes and if you get though too easily he just gets trickier."

"Does that mean…?"

"…that the next question will be more difficult? Yes. I suspect this next one will be a real stinker. But remember if you get it right, you'll be at Level 4."

"And if I don't?"

"Then you've got a bit of a walk in front of you. And you'll have to do it on your own, because I've got an appointment elsewhere."

This is not what you want to hear. If you're left in the Sahara all alone you'll probably die of thirst.

"Okay here it is. Choose carefully now," the boy says. "Do the camels of North Africa, where the Sahara Desert is, have one hump or two?"

"How should I know?" you say. "I'm not an expert on camels!"

"Would you like a hint?" the boy asks.

"Yes please," you say.

"The answer is less than three."

"What! That's a very odd hint."

"Exactly!" the boy says with a big grin. "An odd question indeed."

What is he trying to tell you with this cryptic clue? It's all very odd.

"It is time to make a decision," the boy says. "If you get it right, you'll make it to Level 4. But if you get it wrong. It's back to the beginning of Level 3 for you."

So, which is correct?

Camels of the Sahara have one hump. **P74**

Or

Camels of the Sahara have two humps. **P51**

Oops, that is not the name of a monkey

Would you like to:

Try that question again? **P56**

Or

Go to Level 3? **P51**

60

You have chosen the wrong river

Both the Nile and the Congo are rivers in Africa.

The Nile is the longest river in the world, while the Amazon carries the largest volume of water.

You wish you'd known this before because now you've been sucked up by a swirling tornado and carried up into the sky.

You close your eyes to protect them from the dust and hope the sorcerer drops you somewhere safe. As the tornado spins faster and faster, you fly higher and higher.

Then someone grabs your hand.

It's the boy.

"Did you know tornados can pick up whole trucks and cars and throw them about like toys?" the sorcerer's apprentice yells over the howling wind.

"What? I can't hear you!" you yell back.

Then, as quickly as it started, the wind stops and you're

F
A
L
L
I
N
G

The ground is far below and houses look like pieces of Lego.

"Quickly, pull the rip cord!" the sorcerer's apprentice

yells. "Hurry, or you'll hit the ground with a splat!"

You look down at your chest and see a sturdy metal handle with a cord attached to it.

"Just yank it hard!" the boy yells.

With a tug, the cord releases your parachute and your freefall jerks to a halt. Above you billows a brightly colored parachute.

The boy, hanging below a chute of his own gives you the thumbs up. "That sorcerer's a bit of a comedian at times," he says. "The first time I went through the maze I nearly pooped myself."

"Yeah, the sorcerer's funny all right. Funny in the head if you ask me."

"Now to avoid breaking your legs you're gonna want to bend your knees and roll when you land," the boy says, pulling on his ropes to steer his chute past a fence and into a big field of grass.

You do the same. The ground is coming up fast.

"Oomph," you grunt as you hit the grass and roll.

The boy detaches his harness and runs over to help you with yours. "Wasn't that fun?" he asks.

"Yeah, right. I love being sucked up into the sky and then dropped from a great height when I'm not expecting it."

The boy shrugs. "You get used to it."

"You mean it might happen again?"

"You never know with the sorcerer. In the meantime," the boy says pulling a piece of paper out of his pocket. "The sorcerer wants me to ask you a question."

62

You exhale long and slow. You need to concentrate and get this right so you can get through this crazy maze.

"Right," the boy says. "If you get this correct, you get to start Level 4. But you have to go all the way back to the beginning of Level 3 if you get it wrong.

"Okay you say. What's the question?"

"Right. Who were the first people credited with heavier-than-air powered flight?"

It is time to make a decision. Which is right?

The Boeing Brothers were the first to fly. **P51**

Or

The Wright Brothers were the first to fly. **P74**

You have chosen Venezuela

Well done, you got it right. At a height of 3,212 feet, Angel Falls is in the Canaima National Park in Venezuela. First discovered by Europeans in the 1930s by a pilot named Jimmy Angel.

"So, have you been to Venezuela before?" the sorcerer's apprentice asks.

"Why?" you ask. "Have you got more questions to ask me?

The boy laughs. "How did you know?"

"Just a lucky guess. Doh! Tell me, did the sorcerer use to be a travel agent by any chance?"

The boy shakes his head. "Not that I'm aware of. He does send me around the world a bit though. One of the perks of the job I guess."

"You mean you get paid for doing this?" you ask.

"Well of course. There's a minimum wage law and the sorcerer isn't a criminal."

"So how much do you get an hour?" you say, wondering if there are any vacancies.

"Well I could give you the weekly rate and you could work it out. How's that?"

That seems fair. "Yeah, okay."

"And," the boy says. "If you get this right, you can move on through the maze."

"And if I don't?"

"Well … back to the beginning of Level 2 for you!"

64

You frown at the boy. "Just what I was afraid of."

"Okay here's your question. If I work on a Saturday, I get time and a half. Last Saturday I earned $96 for an eight hour day. What is my normal hourly rate?"

It is time to make a decision. Is the boy's normal hourly rate:

$8.00 per hour **P65**

Or is it:

$12.00 per hour **P25**

(You can use a calculator if required)

You chose $8 per hour

"Well done," the sorcerer's apprentice says. I usually earn 8 dollars an hour but time and a half on a Saturday is $12 per hour and 8 times 12 is 96."

The boy leads you through a thick purple fog. When the fog clears you are standing in the biggest shopping mall you've ever seen and your clothes smell of grape jelly.

"Where did the jungle go?" you ask the sorcerer's apprentice.

"It's back in South America," he replies. "We're in Dubai."

"I've heard of Dubai, but I'm not that sure where that is," you say, looking around at all the shops."

"Well that's okay, because Dubai has nothing to do with the next question. I just came to buy some socks."

"Socks?" you ask.

"The next question is about math. Not socks though," the boy says, popping into a nearby shop.

That is not what you wanted to hear. But at least you figure you'll have a 50/50 chance of getting the next one right.

The boy comes out of the shop holding a small parcel in his hand. "You're probably thinking you've got a 50/50 chance with this next question don't you?" the boy says.

"How do you do that?" you say. "Seems an unfair advantage being able to read my mind."

"It was just an educated guess. Mind reading is just

trickery, it's not real."

You pretend to agree with him, but you're not so sure. "Okay, well let's get it over with. What's the question?"

"This one is more a test in observation. Just pick the number that's different." He points to the glass window of the nearest shop. On it is a list of numbers. "This should be easy. I'll even give you a hint. The correct answer sounds like the German word for no."

Which number in the left hand list is different from the others?

1 **P70**
2 **P67**
3 **P41**
5 **P25**
7 **P70**
9 **P68**
11 **P70**
13 **P67**

You have chosen the wrong number

"If you chose number 2 because it was the only even number, that was a good try," the sorcerer's apprentice says. "But that's not the number I'm looking for. This is a tricky question, you'll have to think harder."

"But is it really tricky, or are you trying to trick me by telling me it's tricky?" you ask.

The boy smiles. "Do you want to try again, or should I just tell you the correct answer?"

Do you:

Try again **P66**

Or

Skip this question and go to the correct answer. **P68**

Or

Take a chance and go to **P70**

You have correctly chosen number 9

Well done. Yes, 9 is different from all the other numbers because it's the only one that isn't a prime number.

What is a prime number?

Well, a prime number is a number than can only be divided by itself and the number 1.

17 is also a prime number. Can you guess which prime number is the one after 17? Remember it won't be an even number (2 is the only even prime number) because you can divide all even numbers by 1 and 2 so it can't be prime.

But if you picked 19 you were right. So that gives us 1, 2, 3, 5, 7, 11, 13, 17, 19 ... they go on and on, but they get harder and harder to find as they get bigger. How many numbers can you find that can only be divided by 1 and the number itself?

In a puff of black smoke, the sorcerer's apprentice arrives. He coughs and his face is covered in soot.

"Where have you been?" you ask. "You're all dirty."

The boy brushes off his clothes and wipes his face with a tissue. "I've been shoveling coal."

"Why?" you ask. "Was the sorcerer punishing you?"

"No the sorcerer was cold and he's got a coal boiler to heat his cave in the winter."

You look at the boy. "But why doesn't he live in a proper house. Surely it would be much warmer than a damp cave?"

"But he quite likes living in a cave," the boys says. "He was born in a cave and he feels he needs to carry on sorcerer traditions."

"But why?" you ask. "Why would he do that when much warmer houses have been made? Just because something's old doesn't make it better. We learn how to do things better all the time. Take medicine for example."

"Speaking of which, the sorcerer has given me a question to ask you. It's about old stuff too."

"Old stuff?"

"Yes. And this is an important one too. If you get it wrong, the sorcerer said he's going to send you all the way back to the very beginning of the maze."

"What? All the way back to Level 1?

"I'm afraid so. The sorcerer likes having you around. He doesn't have many friends."

"But we haven't even met," you say. "How can he like me?"

The boy smiles. "My reports of course."

"Oh well. I suppose you'd better give me the question," you say. "No point in wasting time if I'm going to have to work my way all the way through the maze again."

"Okay, here goes. What is coal made from?"

"The stuff you've been shoveling?" you ask.

"Yep."

It is time for you to make a decision. Which of the following answers is correct?

Coal comes from ancient trees and plants. **P71**

Or

Coal is a type of rock made inside a volcano. **P70**

You are back at the start

In a puff of pink smoke, you find yourself standing on mushy marshmallow. You and the boy bounce from spot to spot avoid sinking in. The sign hanging on the wall says:

YOU ARE AT THE BEGINNING OF THE SORCERER'S MAZE

Down at the end of the hallway is the same ugly old red door.

"I wish I could get a different colored door for a change," you say.

"Be careful what you wish for in the sorcerer's maze," the boy says. "You might get more than you bargained for."

You bounce over to the door and try the handle. Of course it's locked, just like last time. Is it the same question you were asked before? Yes! Well at least you'll know the answer this time.

The questions reads: What is the largest planet in our solar system?

Which one do you choose?

Jupiter? **P4**

Or

Saturn? **P5**

"Would you like to have that last one over again?" the boy says. "I like you. And I am here to help. What do you say?"

If your answer is "Yes" turn back to page**P69**

Coal is made from ancient trees and plants

Well done that is correct. Coal was formed long before the dinosaurs when layers of plant material was laid down in swamps. As the layers were buried they were pressed by the weight of the earth into the coal we burn today. Coal is a very dirty way to get energy and creates lots of greenhouse gasses.

"So now you know a bit about coal," the sorcerer's apprentice says. "But did you know that oil is made from plant material too? That's why they are both called fossil fuels."

"Is that why we're in Texas?"

"Very good," the boys says. "How did you know we've been transported to Texas?"

"The 'Welcome to Texas' sign behind you was a big clue," you say smugly.

The boy turns around. "Oh, I didn't see that. So you're not so clever after all."

"Does that mean my next question is about Texas?" you ask.

"You're getting the hang of this game," the boy says. "Did you know that until Alaska joined the union Texas was the largest state?"

"Yeah I heard that," you say.

"But do you know how the United States got Alaska?"

"Is this my next question?"

The boy nods. "Yes, and if you get it correct, you get to

72

go to the beginning of Level 4. How's that?"

It is time to make a decision. Which of the following is correct?

The U.S. bought Alaska from Russia in 1867. **P74**

Or

Alaska was taken from Japan at the end of World War 2. **P73**

Alaska was taken from Japan at the end of World War 2

Unfortunately, this is incorrect. Alaska was purchased from Russia in 1867 but didn't become a state until 1959.

You look around and wonder where you are. It is suddenly very hot and dry. The ground around you is sandy and there are cattle munching on the sparse grass.

"Where are we now?" you ask the sorcerer's apprentice. "Are we in Texas?"

"Close, but not quite."

"New Mexico?"

The boy shakes his head

"Oklahoma?" you ask.

"Nope."

"Arkansas?" you guess.

"Nope."

"Well we can't be in Mexico because that stop sign over there is in English, not Spanish."

The boy smiles. "There is one more state that borders Texas. If you get this right you get to go to the beginning of Level 4. However if you get it wrong ... well let's not think about that."

It is time to make a decision. Which of these three states borders Texas?

Arizona **P51**

Mississippi **P49**

Or

Louisiana **P74**

Welcome to Level 4

If this is the first time you've been on level 4, you're doing pretty well. If not, welcome back.

The apprentice gives you a smile. "Now you've got some quick decisions to make in the final rush to the end."

You look down the long hallway. It is lined with different colored doors. "What are all the doors for?"

"Only two of them work from this side. All the others can only be opened from the other side." The boy points to the end of the hallway. "To start, you can choose either the red door or the green door."

"And what happens if I choose wrong?" you ask.

"Well you'll be in this part of the maze for quite some time. Try to remember your path and you might make it out again."

"Aren't you coming with me?"

The boy shakes his head. "I've got other work to do. From here on it's up to you."

You walk down the hallway past doors of various colors.

Finally you come to a red door and a green door. You turn around to wave goodbye to the boy, but when you look back, he's already gone.

You scratch your head.

Which door do you choose? Does green mean go and red mean stop? Or is this another one of the sorcerer's tricks?"

It is time to make a decision. Which door do you open?

Open the red door. **P76**

Or

Open the green door. **P77**

You have chosen the red door

You are in near darkness. The walls are slimy. It smells like a sewer. You hear the squeak of rats and feel something scurrying around your feet.

The ground at your feet is hard like concrete. You run from the rats. Finally you turn a corner. In front of you are two doors. One is yellow and one is orange.

More rats have found you. They are getting bolder, coming closer.

Quick, which door do you take?

Take the yellow door. **P78**

Or

Take the orange door. **P79**

You have chosen the green door

Behind the green door is a dark room with a jungle scene painted on its walls. You look around for some more doors, but they are disguised. You hear a deep throated roar, but when you look around you can't see where the noise is coming from.

You reach out and run your hands along the wall. Maybe you'll be able to feel the knob? You start moving around the walls feeling for as you go, but after a few minutes you give up.

Then you spot something interesting. There are two little buttons painted to look like tiny flowers.

One of the buttons says UP, and the other says DOWN.

You take a moment to think. Then you see a tiger sitting quietly in the corner. The tiger is staring at you. It licks its lips and stands up. It moves towards you … stalking you.

Quick, push a button!

Do you:

Push the up button? **P80**

Or

Push the down button? **P81**

You have chosen the yellow door

Beyond the yellow door is a long hallway lined with mirrors. You see your reflection and it seems to go on forever.

After walking down the hallway, you come to a junction. You turn right and keep walking. You seem to be walking in circles but then, finally you see two doors in the distance. A blue door and a purple door.

But which door do you take?

Take the blue door. **P83**

Or

Take the purple door. **P82**

You have chosen the orange door

You are in a round room with blue and white tiles on the floor. What a strange place. On the walls are a series of pipes protruding into the room. On the wall are two doors, one pink and one brown.

What should you do? You are starting to wish there were questions to answer because choosing doors is just luck.

As you think about which door to choose, water starts to pour out of the pipes. This room must be a swimming pool, but there is a roof on it. What happens when the pool fills up? There won't be any air left.

The water is gushing in faster and faster. It is cold and already up to your neck. Quick, before you drown! Choose a door!

Open the pink door. **P83**

Or

Open the brown door. **P86**

You have pushed the up button

After pushing the UP button, a sliding door opens. You rush inside and hide from the tiger. Thankfully the door closes again just before the tiger pounces. You hear the tiger's claws scratching on the outside of the door as the lift takes off.

Siberian tigers can weigh up to 675 pounds. You wouldn't last long if one of those got hold of you.

The elevator travels up and up. Finally it stops and the doors open again

"Oh no!" you cry out. "I've gone around in a circle!"

You are back in the hallway of doors.

Looks like it time to start again. So which door do you take this time?

The green door? **P77**

Or

The red door? **P76**

You have pushed the down button

After pushing the down button, a sliding door opens. You jump inside the lift and the doors slam shut just as the tiger leaps towards you.

Down, down, and down you go. Then with a jerk, you come to a stop. But the door doesn't open.

You wait for a while longer, but still the door doesn't open. What are you going to do?

The only button on the inside of the lift is an UP button, but there is a tiger up there. You don't want to go up again surely?

Then you see them. A trap door in the floor of the lift and another tiny door in the back wall that is only as high as your knees.

What do you do? Do you:

Go through the trap door? **P88**

Or

Go through the tiny door? **P83**

You have chosen the purple door

You're standing in a long metal box. It is cold and there is ice on the walls. The floor is a little sloped and you are sliding downhill, not quickly, but because you've got nothing to hold on to, you can't stop.

You hold out your arms to keep your balance as you slide.

Then you see a metal ladder attached to the wall. Above the ladder, there is a trap door in the ceiling. Opposite the ladder is a round porthole with a big metal handle, like those you'd see in a submarine.

It is freezing. Your arms are covered in goose bumps.

You need to choose quickly before you turn into ice. Do you:

Climb the ladder? **P84**

Or

Open the porthole? **P83**

You are back in the hallway of doors

How did that happen? You must have taken a wrong turn somewhere.

You look around but the sorcerer's apprentice is nowhere to be seen.

Looks like you're starting over again.

You walk down the long hallway. Past door after door. Only two of them have doorknobs.

Which door do you take?

The green door? **P77**

Or

The red door? **P76**

You have chosen to climb the ladder

You open the trap door at the top of the ladder and haul yourself up. You find yourself in a long narrow passageway. The walls are covered in spiders. Hundreds of big brown hairy spiders. Some of them skitter towards you. You try to go back, but the trap door has shut and there is no handle on this side. What are you going to do?

Then, down at the end of the hallway you see two doors. You run, brushing spiders off you as you go.

One of the doors is red the other is black. Just like the colors of a black widow spider. But which do you choose?

Quick the spiders are getting closer! Choose a door!

Choose the red door. **P76**

Or

Choose the black door. **P85**

You have chosen the black door

You smell pizza as soon as you enter the next room and slam the black door shut. The room is large with a big window in one wall. On the other side of the window the sorcerer's apprentice is eating pizza with 5 others. Two of them are twins. It feels like you've been here before.

It's been hours since you've had any food.

You knock on the window but nobody can hear you. There are no doors that you can see but at the end of the room is a hole in the wall. Maybe that is the way to get out of this maze.

As you walk towards the hole, you see a trap door in the floor. Maybe the trap door is the better way to go?

It is time to make a decision. Do you:

Go through the hole in the wall? **P93**

Or

Go down through the trap door? **P88**

86

You have chosen the brown door

You can still hear water running behind you. A few drops seep under the brown door even though it's closed firmly behind you.

It is gloomy in this room. Then you see a light switch on the wall beside you. You turn it on.

Oh no! There are doors everywhere. And if that wasn't bad enough, it smells horrible. Like a hundred people have farted all at the same time!

You try to hold your breath, but you know you need to get out as soon as possible.

But which of the six doors do you choose?

Green **P77**

Red **P76**

Yellow **P78**

Purple **P82**

White **P87**

Blue **P83**

You have chosen the white door

This is the longest hallway you've seen yet. It seems to go on forever. As you walk you see pictures of the boy doing different activities. In one picture he is parachuting, in another he is standing on top of a mountain. In the next, he is standing at the foot of a massive waterfall, and at another, he is playing with a long-armed monkey up in a tree.

Then you notice that you're in some of the pictures too. What is going on here?

After walking for ten minutes, you finally see a couple of doors. One has yellow dots on it. The other has blue stripes. Then music starts to play. It sounds like a circus is in town.

Which door do you choose?

Choose the door with the yellow spots. **P83**

Or

Choose the door with the blue stripes. **P89**

You have decided to go through the trap door

The air is cool down here. The walls are made of stone and there are burning torches every few yards along the passageway so you can see where you are going.

At the end of the passage stands a shiny suit of armor, complete with spear. It looks about your size. You wonder if the sorcerer has put it there for a reason, or if it's just decoration. Beside the armor lays a double-edged axe.

When you see a sign that says BEWARE OF THE DRAGON you start to worry.

Maybe you should put the suit on, but then how? You'd need someone to help you do up the back.

Instead you pick up the axe and creep slowly forward.

At the end of the passageway are two huge doors, one of wood and one covered in beaten copper.

When you hear the hiss of the dragon behind you, you realize you've got to move quickly. Flames lick around your feet. You drop the axe and run towards the doors. But which do you open?

The wooden door? **P74**

Or

The copper door? **P91**

Go through the door with the blue stripes

Now you seem to be getting somewhere.

You find yourself in a luxurious room filled with plush furniture.

There is a big screen TV on one wall and a fridge in the corner. You're over to the fridge in a flash to see what's inside.

You reach into the freezer compartment and grab a popsicle.

As you eat, the TV flickers to life. You see an old white-haired man on the screen dressed in colorful robes.

"Can you hear me?" the man on the TV says.

"Are you talking to me?" you ask.

"Yes, I'm taking to you."

"Are you the sorcerer?" you ask.

"No, I am the sorcerer's grandfather."

"Can you tell me how to get out of this maze?"

The old man shakes his head. "No, but I can tell you that in a few moments a whole lot of doors are going to appear and you will have to choose one of them."

"More doors?"

"I'm afraid so."

Then the TV turns off again.

When you turn around, sure enough six doors have appeared.

But which one do you choose?

There are so many.

90

Do you choose the:
Red door **P76**
Purple door **P82**
Orange door **P79**
Wooden door **P83**
Copper door **P91**
Yellow door **P74**

You have chosen to open the copper door

"Hello again," the sorcerer's apprentice says. "Did you miss me?"

"A bit?" you say. "It seems to have taken ages to get here. I took a few wrong turns."

"Well you've done better than most, so don't complain."

"So what now?" you ask. "Have I got far to go?"

"No not at all," the boy says. "This is the last stage. If you get this right, you might get to meet the sorcerer."

"I'm not sure I want to meet him after all he's put me through," you say. "So, is this the last question?"

"How did you guess?" the boy says.

You sigh preparing for what surely must be the hardest question of all.

"Ready?"

You nod.

"Good luck!"

"Thanks."

"Right. How many cards are in a pack of playing cards, not counting the jokers?"

"Just regular playing cards?" you ask.

The boy nods and gives you a big grin. "Think hard," the boys says.

"Don't worry I will," you reply.

"Work it out by going through the pack if you have to. If you get this wrong ... well I suspect you know what will happen. You'll be back at the very beginning of the maze

92

and have to start over."

You take your time before you answer.

"Remember there are four suits," the apprentice says.

It is time to answer. Are there:

50 cards in a pack? **P83**

Or

52 cards in a pack? **P95**

You have decided to go through the hole in the wall

The hole is dark and you can't see much. You walk forward slowly, feeling the way as you go. The wall feels cold and rough like rock. You wonder if you've entered a cave.

As you walk, it gets warmer and warmer. Where have you ended up?

There is a rumbling beneath your feet. It's an earthquake.

When you see lava running down the tunnel towards you, you realize you're in a lava tube and the volcano is erupting! You've got to get out of here fast!

You turn and run wondering where to go.

Then you see a junction you didn't see on the way in. You must have passed it in the gloom.

Lava hisses behind you. You can feel its heat on your back.

Which way do you go? Do you:

Go left? **P74**

Or

Go right? **P94**

You have decided to go right

As you head further down the tunnel the floor gets steeper and steeper. Before you know it, you are running so fast you're not sure you could stop even if you wanted to.

Thankfully, after another fifty yards the tunnel levels out and comes to an end. You can hear the sizzling lava behind you. But where can you go? What can you do?

A voice booms through the tunnel. "Look up!"

Then you see it. A rope is hanging from the ceiling. It has big knots tied in it to help you climb up. You grab hold and start climbing just as the lava flows under you.

It is hot. Your hands sweat as you climb. You feel like you're about to be roasted alive when you come to a small ledge with two doors set back into it.

One of the doors is made of silver and shines brightly in the light. The other looks like solid gold.

But which do you choose? Do you:

Go through the door made silver? **P74**

Or

Go through the door made of gold? **P95**

Congratulations, you made it to the end of the maze

The last room is like nothing you've ever seen. Shelves of books tower to the sky. High above, a flock of birds circle amongst the clouds.

In the middle of the room the boy sits at a large desk. He is dressed in colorful robes and has a pointy cap on. A jumble of books are open on the desk in front of him.

"I'm pleased to see you finally made it," he says.

You nod and then look around. "So where's the sorcerer?"

The boy snaps his fingers. "Abracadabra!" In a puff of pink smoke, a box of chocolates plops onto the desk in front of you. "Like some chocolate?"

You look at his beaming grin. "You mean you were the sorcerer all along?"

He waves his wand and a big leather chair appears. "Please take a seat and I'll explain."

The chair is huge and soft, like sitting on a cloud.

"Sorry for deceiving you, but I need more apprentices. You see I have so many mazes to make I'm having to do 100 jobs at once."

You could get angry, but what's the point. Besides, the chocolates are the best you've ever tasted. "So why didn't you tell me the truth from the beginning?" you ask.

The boy smiles. "I wanted you to see how much fun it is being an apprentice. You'd have gotten all nervous if you knew I was the sorcerer."

You think back to all the adventures you've had. "It was kind of fun. But why did you care?"

The sorcerer gives you a serious look as he leans forward. "I was hoping you might like to become an apprentice." He snaps his fingers and a fluffy kitten lands on your lap. "There are lots of perks you know and to tell you the truth, I could really do with some help."

You must admit you're interested. Going through the maze was a lot of fun and becoming one of the sorcerer's apprentices would be exciting. "What would I have to do?"

"You'd help make up the questions for my maze. And every now and then you get to act as guide for someone new. Like I did for you as you went through."

"I can think of lots of cool questions," you say. "Did you know that lava can get up to 1100 degrees Celsius?"

"Hmm… interesting," he says. "You sound like a natural."

The sorcerer stands up. "Look, you don't have to make your mind up right now. Have a think about it and if you want to apply for the job let me know. You can apply at my website. You know, I think we could become good friends."

You grab another chocolate and give the kitten a pat.

"I'd better get back to work," the sorcerer says. "I've a million interesting facts to look up."

And with that, the sorcerer disappears. In a puff of marshmallow smelling smoke you find yourself back at home, smarter than you were when you left. You find yourself thinking of all the interesting questions and riddles you'll make up if you decide to become the sorcerer's apprentice.

THE END

Why not check out the List of Choices on the next page and make sure you've not missed anything important. Or if you'd prefer to go right on to the next story go to **P103**.

List of Choices

THE SORCERER'S MAZE TIME MACHINE

(Book Two)

In the laboratory

The door is ajar so Matilda gives it a shove and walks into the laboratory. "Hey," she says over her shoulder, "come and look at this."

"Are we allowed?" you ask, stepping cautiously through the doorway. "This area's probably off limits."

"I didn't see a sign," Matilda says, rubbing a finger along the edge of a stainless steel bench as she proceeds further into the brightly lit room. "And if they're going to leave the door open…"

Matilda is an Australian foreign exchange student at your school. She's adventurous and sometimes a little crazy, but she's interesting and the two of you have become good friends.

The rest of your classmates are back in the cafeteria questioning the tour guide about the research facility while they wait for lunch to be served. When Matilda suggested a quick walk, you never guessed she planned to snoop around.

The lab's benches are crammed with electrical equipment. Wires and cables run like spaghetti between servers and fancy hardware. Lights and gauges flicker and glow.

You move a little further into the room. "What do you think all this stuff does?"

Matilda wanders down the narrow space between two benches, looking intently at the equipment as she goes. "I dunno. But they don't skimp on gear, do they?"

A low hum buzzes throughout the room. Most of the components are large and expensive looking. But near the end of one bench, Matilda spots a few smaller pieces of tech.

She prods a brick-sized black box with a row of green numbers glowing across it. "I wonder what this does." She picks it up.

Tiny lights glow above a circular dial. On the top of the box is an exposed circuit board made of copper and green plastic.

"Looks like an old digital clock," you say pointing at the first number in the row. "See here's the hours and minutes, then the day, the month and the year." You pull out your cell phone and check the time. "Yep. It's spot on."

"That makes sense," Matilda says. "But what's the dial for?"

"Beats me. To set an alarm, maybe?

Matilda rubs her finger along a curved piece of copper tubing fitted neatly into one end of the box. "So what's this coil for? Doesn't look like any timer I've ever seen."

When she turns the box over, there is a sticky label on its bottom. It reads:

Hands Off - Property of the Sorcerer

"Who's the sorcerer?" Matilda asks.

You shrug. "A scientist maybe?"

"A sorcerer's a magician, not a scientist." She turns the box back over and starts fiddling with the dial.

You take a step back. "I don't think that's a good—"

A sudden burst of static crackles through the air. The copper coil glows bright red and there's a high-pitched squeal.

FLASH—BANG!

Pink mist fills the air.

"Crikey!" Matilda says. "What the heck caused that?"

Matilda looms ghostlike through the haze.

"We're in for it now," you say, hoping the smoke alarm doesn't go off. "Someone must have heard that."

But as the mist clears, someone hearing you is the last of your worries. "Where—where's the lab gone?"

You're standing on an open plain, brown and burnt by the blistering sun.

In the distance three huge stone structures rise above the shimmering heat haze. Workers swarm over the site like ants on piles of sugar.

Matilda stares, her mouth open, trying to make sense of it all. The black box dangles from her hand. She turns to face you. "Streuth mate! The lab. She—she's completely disappeared!"

"But how? Unless…" You reach down and lift the box so you can check the numbers flashing on its side. "This says it's 11:45."

Matilda nods. "Yeah, that's about right. Just before lunch."

"In the year 2560!"

Matilda's eyes widen. "2560? How can that be?"

"That's 2560 BC," a voice behind you says. "See the little minus sign in front of the numbers?"

The two of you spin around.

"Jeez, mate," Matilda says, glaring at the newcomer.

"Where the blazes did you spring from? You nearly scared last night's dinner outta me."

The owner of the voice is a boy about your age, dressed in white cotton.

Bands of gold encircle his wrists. His hair is jet black and cut straight across in the front, like his barber put a bowl on his head and used it as a guide.

"I'm the sorcerer's apprentice," he says with a smile. "You've been playing with the sorcerer's time machine haven't you?"

"Time machine?" you and Matilda say in unison.

The apprentice nods. "Welcome to ancient Egypt. The pyramids are coming along nicely don't you think?"

You glance over towards the structures in the distance then back to the boy. "But how did we—"

"— end up here?" the apprentice says. "When you fiddled with the sorcerer's machine, you bent space-time. In fact you bent it so much, you've ended up in the sorcerer's maze. Now you've got to answer questions and riddles to get out."

Matilda's upper lip curls and her eyes squint, contorting her face into a look of total confusion. "What sorta questions?"

The apprentice reaches out his hand. "Don't worry. The questions aren't difficult. But first you'd better give me that box, before you get yourself in trouble."

"Is answering questions the only way to get back?" you ask.

The boy in white nods then gives you a smile. "Here's how the time maze works. If you answer a question correctly, you get to move closer to your own time. But if you get it wrong. I spin the dial and we take our chances."

You gulp. "You mean we could end up anywhere?"

"You mean any-when, don't ya?" Matilda says.

The sorcerer's apprentice chuckles. "I suppose you're right. Anywhere, anytime. It's all the same in the sorcerer's maze."

"But we've got to answer questions to get home?" you repeat. "There's no other way?"

"Sorry, I don't make the rules. I just do what the sorcerer says. At least he's sent me along to help out. That's some consolation, eh?"

"Well… I suppose…"

"Get on with it then," Matilda says in her typical no-nonsense way. "I'm hungry and it's nearly lunchtime."

The boy tucks the black box under his arm, then reaches into a fold of his robe and pulls out a scroll of papyrus. He straightens the scroll and reads. "Okay here goes. The pyramids are about 481 feet high but they weren't used as look out posts or land marks. What was their purpose?" The apprentice looks at you expectantly.

It's time for your first decision. Which do you choose?

The pyramids were used as accommodation for slaves? **P111**

Or

The pyramids were used as tombs? **P114**

110

Stop. You need to go back and make a choice. That is how you'll work your way through the sorcerer's maze.

The pyramids were used as accommodation for slaves

"Oops," the sorcerer's apprentice says. "I'm afraid to say that isn't the right answer. But don't worry, we'll spin the dial and see where we end up eh? Pity I was hoping to have a little look at how the Egyptians lifted up those big blocks of stone.

The boy reaches for the dial on the front of the box.

"Hey wait!" you shout. "You sure you couldn't give me another chance?"

The boy shakes his head. "If it were up to me, I wouldn't have a problem. But I don't make the rules."

He spins the dial. The air crackles.

FLASH—BANG!

That pink mist is back. You wave you hand in front of your face to fan it away.

"Crikey!" Matilda says, fanning like crazy. "Look over there! It's the Eiffel Tower!"

She's right. You'd know that shape anywhere.

You turn to the sorcerer's apprentice. "But—but where's the top of it?

"The French haven't finished it yet," the sorcerer's apprentice says.

He's now dressed in a black frock coat that hangs nearly to his knees. Under the coat charcoal-colored pin-striped pants meet shiny black shoes with silver buckles. On top of his head is a top hat, and he carries a cane. He studies the front of the box and points at the last four numbers. "See, it's only 1888."

"1888?" you say. "At least we're closer to home. That's good."

The boy smiles, "Did you know that the four legs of the tower point north, south, east and west?"

"Like a compass?" Matilda asks.

The apprentice nods "It's being built for the Exposition Universelle of 1889. It won't be finished until March next year."

"Exposition Univer—"

"—it's like a World Fair," the boys says. "Did you know the Eiffel Tower has over two and half million rivets?"

You remember reading something about that. "Didn't the French build the Statue of Liberty too?"

"That's right," the apprentice says. "So, are you ready for another question?"

"Heck yeah," Matilda says. "My stomach's rumbling. We haven't had lunch yet."

"Okay, here we go," the boy says, pulling a piece of paper from his coat pocket. "In what year was George Washington, the first president of the United States, elected?"

"Jeez mate. How am I supposed to know that?" Matilda moans. "Why don't ya ask us something 'bout Australia? Then I might be able to help."

The boy smiles. "Maybe. But hey, even a guess has a 50/50 chance."

Then he turns to you. "Which do you choose?"

Washington was elected in 1689? **P117**

Or

Washington was elected in 1789? **P119**

114

The pyramids were used as tombs

"Well done," the sorcerer's apprentice says. "That's correct. The pyramids were used as burial chambers for Egyptian kings and queens. They were filled with all the things the Egyptians believed people would need in the afterlife."

Matilda gives you a smile. "I knew that."

"So what now?" you ask the boy. "We get to head towards home, right?"

"Don't you want to look around?" the boy asks.

"Can we get some food?" Matilda says. "My stomach is rumbling."

"I'm pretty sure we can find something," the boy says.

But then, out of the haze, a group of Egyptian men armed with spears, come running towards you.

They are shouting words you can't understand and they

don't look friendly.

The boy nods and reaches towards the dial on the black box. "I think we'd better get going. How about 1863?"

"Is that an important date?" Matilda asks, casting a glance at the approaching men. "It sounds familiar."

"You'll see," the apprentice says. "You might want to put your hands over your ears," the boy says. "These bangs can damage your hearing after a while."

FLASH—BANG!

Egypt is gone. As the pink cloud thins, you see a big white house across a large expanse of lawn. Two white pillars sit either side of the entrance.

"This mist tastes like cherry," Matilda says, licking her lips. "Yummo!"

You ignore Matilda as she slurps at the air. "So is this 1863?" you ask.

"That's right," the apprentice says. "We're in Washington D.C."

"So that's the White House?" Matilda asks.

"Very good," the apprentice says. "Guess who's president?"

You shrug. "How should I know? That was a long time ago."

"It was Lincoln," the apprentice says, "And what did Abraham Lincoln do that people remember him for?"

"Hang on mate!" Matilda says. "If we're going to answer your questions, we should get to move closer to home. Otherwise we're working for nothing."

116

"Okay," the apprentice says. "Tell me what Lincoln was famous for and we'll turn the dial nearer your own time. Was it:"

Being the first president to send a man into space? **P121**

Or

Being the president that ended slavery in the United States? **P123**

Washington was elected in 1689

The sorcerer's apprentice frowns. "How could George Washington have been elected in 1689 when the *Declaration of Independence* wasn't signed until 1776? You didn't think that one through did you?"

Matilda frowns. "Hey mate! How were we supposed to know that? It's ancient history. Give us something a bit more recent why don't ya?"

"Yeah," you agree. "Give us a chance or we'll never get home."

The sorcerer's apprentice scratches his head. "Okay, I suppose questions from that long ago are a bit unfair. I'll tell you what. If you promise not to tell the sorcerer. I'll let you have that one over again."

Matilda smiles and gives the apprentice a thumbs up

signal. "Cheers, mate. You're a good sort."

The apprentice reads the last question over. "So which do you choose this time?"

Washington was elected in 1689 **P117**

Or

Washington was elected in 1789? **P119**

Washington was elected in 1789

"Correct," the apprentice says. "How could Washington have been elected in 1689? That's before the United States was even a country."

Matilda gives you a toothy grin. "Good picking, cobber!"

The apprentice turns to you for a translation.

"Cobber means friend," you say.

The sorcerer's apprentice files the information away for future use and then continues his history lesson. "Did you know that Washington served as general and commander-in-chief in the War of Independence against the British, and that he was a slave owner?"

"Really?" you ask. "A slave owner while he was president?"

"Of course we know better now," the apprentice says.

120

Matilda kicks the ground. "So where are we off to now? I don't suppose they've invented hamburgers yet?"

The sorcerer's apprentice smiles. "No. That wasn't until the 1880s in Texas."

"Well that's closer to our time," Matilda says, turning to you. "What do you reckon?"

You must admit, a burger and fries sounds pretty good right now. "Can we?" you ask the apprentice.

"Sure we can," he says. "Or we can go to 2040. That's a little bit past your time, but it's closer."

"Bleeding heck!" Matilda says. "You mean we can go into the future too?"

The sorcerer's apprentice nods. "But do you want to risk it?" he says with a big grin.

Matilda gives the apprentice a serious look. "Will they have hamburgers in the future too?"

The apprentice grins. "They might."

It is time to make a decision. Which do you choose?

Go to Texas 1880 for burgers? **P126**

Or

Go check out the future? **P134**

Lincoln sent the first man into space

Everything is dark, and the air is thick with the smell of unwashed bodies. Where are Matilda and the boy? "Hello? Anyone there?"

You hear the hollow slap of water against wood.

As your eyes adjust to the dim light, you see vague shapes lying around the floor. You feel yourself rocking to and fro. The stench is horrible. People moan and groan all around you.

"Hello?" you say again. "Matilda? Apprentice? Are you here?"

"Crikey, it stinks worse that the south end of a north-bound dingo," Matilda says. "Get us out of here!"

People mumble in a language you can't understand and water drips on you from above.

"Well that was clever," the boy says from the gloom. "We've ended up in the hold of a slave ship."

"Why?" you ask.

"Because you got that last question wrong! Lincoln abolished slavery in 1862. Man didn't go into space until 1961. What were you thinking?"

You're quite pleased you haven't have lunch. The smell is so bad you'd only throw it up anyway. It's no wonder so many slaves died on the voyage across the Atlantic Ocean, this place is disgusting, and heart breaking.

"Can you ask another question so we can get everyone out of here?" you ask the apprentice.

122

The boy shakes his head. "Unfortunately no. I'm going to leave, but you have to stay here. Slaves can't just run away. They are trapped for life, and so are you.

"What do you mean? We have to stay here?" you ask in a panic. "Can't you take us with you?"

"Bleedin' heck! You must be joking!" Matilda yells.

"I'm sorry. You've made a bad decision. There's nothing I can do.

The air crackles with electricity. Then there's a FLASH—BANG and the apprentice is gone.

"So what do we do now?" Matilda says.

"I don't—" You see a familiar shape on the floor and reach for it. "Look Matilda, the time machine. He must have dropped it." You lift it to your face and peer at the numbers on its front. You fiddle with the dial. "It's jammed! I can only get two dates."

"Just pick one! Anywhere's got to be better than here," she says.

So which date do you choose?

Do you pick the year 1980? **P129**

Or

Do you pick the year 2040? **P134**

Lincoln ended slavery in the U.S.

The sorcerer's apprentice gives you a smile. "That's right. Slavery officially ended in the United States when the 13th amendment to the constitution was passed in 1865. Now we get to move closer to your time."

"Hey, mate," Matilda says to the apprentice. "How about sending us somewhere interesting for a change? All this history is boring me rigid."

The apprentice shoots Matilda a look, and then turns towards you. "Is that how you feel too?"

You're not sure how to react. Is this a trick? Will the apprentice send you off somewhere dangerous if you say something wrong? "Well I'm not sure…"

The apprentice tucks the black box under his arm and reaches for his pocket. "I'll tell you what, get this next question right and we'll go somewhere you're both sure to like. Sound fair?"

You nod. "Sounds fair."

The apprentice holds up the questions and starts to read. "Wow, this one's a bit tricky."

"Really? Can't you give us an easy one?" you ask.

The apprentice shakes his head. "Sorry, I've got to read them as they come out."

"Well get it over with then, mate." Matilda growls. "No point hanging around like a bad smell."

"Yeah, at least we have a 50/50 chance of getting it right," you say.

"Not this time," the apprentice says, shaking his head slightly. "More like a 25 percent chance. There are four possible answers."

Matilda frowns. "Jeez, mate. That's lower than a snake's armpit."

The apprentice looks at Matilda, then to you. "Translation?"

"Mean trick. She's not happy."

"Well I can't help what comes out of my pocket. Still, if you get this one right, you can go have ice cream. That should cheer you both up.

"And if we get it wrong?" you ask

"You're in for a surprise. Now think carefully and tell me what a 'spiny lumpsucker' is?"

"A spiny lumpsucker?" you say. "Is that really a thing?"

"Sure is," the apprentice says.

You can almost see the steam coming out of Matilda's ears. "What the heck's a spiny lumpsucker?"

"Exactly my question," the apprentice says, turning to you. "So, what do you say? Oh but be careful. If you answer wrong, I'll have to send you back to the start or way off into the future. But, if you get it right, you'll get ice cream!"

Your stomach rumbles. "Oh yum!"

It is time to make a decision. Is a spiny lumpsucker:

A type of frog? **P105**

A piece of medical equipment? **P134**

A type of fish? **P152**

Or

A slave owner? **P165**

Have a Texan hamburger

When the pink mist clears you feel the sun beating down. The day is hot and dry. You are standing outside a lunch bar in Athens, Texas. The wind whistles down a near empty street.

"Welcome to 1860," the sorcerer's apprentice says, tipping his cowboy hat. "Ya'll come on in and grab some food." He points to a set of swinging doors that lead into a modest restaurant. Inside, wooden stools line a long counter, and sawdust covers the floor.

As you enter, a dark-haired man with a large moustache stands behind the counter. "Howdy folks," he says.

"We'd like to order some lunch," the apprentice says.

"Sure, no problem. Would you like to try my newest invention?" the man says. "I call it the hamburger."

"I'm in," you say.

The three of you sit along the counter. The smell of food cooking makes your mouth water.

"I'm so hungry I could eat road kill," Matilda says, licking her lips.

The man behind the counter looks confused. "Road kill?"

"Thank you, mister," the sorcerer's apprentice says, distracting the man. "We'll have three of your hamburgers please. And some water if we may."

"All righty then. Three hamburgers a comin' up."

After the man goes out back, the apprentice turns to Matilda. "Road kill in 1860? Do you think they run over rabbits with their horses?"

Matilda's face reddens. "Yeah, well…"

The man is back with three glasses of water. "Here you go," the man says, inspecting your clothes. "You kids aren't from around these parts, are you?"

"I'm from Australia," Matilda says. "I'm going to school—"

"—her parents are teachers over in Austin," the apprentice says, butting in.

The man twiddles his moustache. "Australia. Yeah I heard of that. Knew a man headed there to search for gold."

The man goes to the grill and gets busy frying up three juicy patties. Once they've had time to cook, he puts each patty between two thick slabs of bread with fried onion and adds slices of pickle to decorate the side of the plate.

Matilda's eyes widen.

The burgers are so big, and the bread so thick, you wonder if you'll even be able to finish yours.

Matilda has no such doubt and digs right in.

A while later, the three of you are licking your fingers and wiping your hands on cloth napkins. The sorcerer's apprentice pulls a question out of his pocket. "I suppose we'd better get going before someone else gets nosey. You ready for your next question?"

You burp loudly then nod. "Sure. Go for it."

The apprentice reaches for a question. "Ahem…" he says clearing his throat. "Right, here we go. Which of the following is the correct spelling for Matilda's homeland? Be

128

careful with this one, because you might have to go back to the very beginning of the maze if you get it wrong."

Is it:

Austrialia? **P191**

Australia? **P129**

Or

Australea? **P105**

A land down under

As the mist clears, a dusty red landscape surrounds you. Scrubby trees with narrow leaves dot the countryside. It's hot and flies buzz around your face.

You swat a fly off your cheek. "Where are we?" you ask the sorcerer's apprentice.

"Crikey, ya wombat. Don't ya know?" Matilda says, rolling her eyes skyward. "We're in Australia! How good is that!"

Matilda is so happy, she's hopping around like it's Christmas morning.

You point off in the distance to a massive lump of red rock. "What's that?"

"Ayers rock," Matilda answers. "World's largest sandstone monolith. Over 1000 feet high and two miles long. She's a beauty eh?"

"It's pretty impressive," you say, "for a rock."

The sorcerer's apprentice chuckles. "If I'd known you were going to be so excited, Matilda, I'd have brought you here sooner."

"As long as we don't have to eat goanna," you say, screwing up your face. "Or kangaroo."

"Nothing wrong with barbecued roo," Matilda says.

You give her a doubtful look. "Let me guess. It tastes like chicken."

Matilda throws her head back and snorts. Then she gives you a withering look. "Jeez mate, you must be the world's only living brain donor! Tastes like chicken … ha! Now that's funny."

The sorcerer's apprentice brushes the flies away from his mouth before speaking. "Kangaroo taste a bit like beef and a bit like venison. Now crocodile — that tastes like chicken."

"Fishy chicken, to be exact," Matilda chimes in. "It's good with chips. Or, as you lot call them, French fries."

"Really? You've eaten crocodile?" Before your mouth closes again, a big fat blowfly lands on your tongue. "Pwwwaaa!" you spit. "Oh yuk. How do you put up with all these flies?"

"Just swallow them mate — good protein," Matilda says. "They taste like chicken!" This sets her off cackling like a crazy person. When she stops laughing, she shakes her head. "I'm joking — just keep your mouth shut when you're not talking. That'll help for a start."

"I hate to interrupt your talk about Australian cuisine, but you've got questions to answer. There's still a long way to go to get through the maze."

You point at the rock. "Can we go and climb it? The view from up there must be amazing." you say.

The apprentice shakes his head. "Ayers rock, or Uluru as the local Aborigines call it, is a sacred place. It would be disrespectful to climb it. But the sun will be setting soon. We could stay and watch the rock change color. It's a beautiful sight. Or, if you'd rather do something else, there's a special place I could take you."

"Where's that?" you ask.

"Now that would be telling. Don't you like surprises?"

It is time to make a decision. Do you:

Play it safe and watch the sunset? **P132**

Or

Take a chance and go for a surprise? **P152**

Stay and watch the sunset

"I like the idea of taking it easy and watching the rock change color," you say. "I've already had enough surprises for one day."

The apprentices nods slowly in understanding, then snaps his fingers. Three camp chairs appear. "We may as well be comfortable," he says.

You and Matilda sit and gaze towards the orange rock. It's shaped a bit like a huge loaf of bread with sloping ends. Eucalypts and stunted shrubs dot the flat land around it. As time passes and the sun lowers in the sky, the rock gets redder and redder. The light blue sky becomes darker and the horizon on either side of the rock becomes various shades of pink and lilac.

The rock is a hypnotic sight as the sound of the insects gradually fades.

Before you know it, the sun is gone and the sky is dark. Stars twinkle and the Milky Way runs across the sky like a vast river of light.

"Wow," you say. "I've never seen so many stars."

"It helps being over 200 miles away from the nearest town, and even Katherine isn't very big." the apprentice says. "No light pollution to spoil the view."

"She's a top spot," Matilda says. "But I'm getting hungry. Any chance of snapping up some tucker?"

"Tucker?" the apprentice asks, looking at you.

"Food," you translate.

You can see the apprentices white teeth glisten in the gloom. "I could probably rustle up some ice cream," he says.

"You beauty!" Matilda says.

The apprentice shoots you a glance.

"She likes the idea," you say. "I do too."

The apprentice chuckles. "But first—"

"—I'll need to answer a question," you interrupt.

"How did you guess?" The apprentice chuckles and reaches for his pocket. "If you get this right, you'll get a treat. But if you get it wrong, you might find yourself in the freezer yourself."

"In the freezer?" you ask. "That sounds uncomfortable."

The apprentice shrugs. "So is getting trampled by prehistoric animals."

Now you're really confused.

"Just ask the question, mate!" Matilda shouts. "Can't you see I'm hanging out for ice cream over here?"

"Okay, okay. Keep your hair on," the apprentice says.

"Not too hard please," you say. "I didn't pack a coat."

The apprentice unfolds a small piece of paper. "Okay, seeing this is a time-travel maze. How many seconds are there in one hour?"

Which is correct? Are there:

3,600 seconds in one hour? **P152**

Or

1400 seconds in one hour? **P199**

You have been sent to the future

"Surprise!" the sorcerer's apprentice says. "Welcome to the future."

When the pink mist clears, you find yourself sitting at a long counter in a strange restaurant. Behind the counter, a stainless steel bench runs the length of the wall. In its centre is a gas grill. Beside the grill, a glass beaker filled with thick orange liquid bubbles in a Bunsen burner. The rest of the bench is covered in racks of test tubes, numerous glass beakers, funnels, and other equipment.

"They do good burgers here in 2040," the apprentice says. "The beef is grown in the lab. Very tender."

Matilda frowns. "But I don't want a hamburger grown in some Petri dish. That sounds gross!"

The cook behind the counter shakes her head and wipes

her hands on her apron. "It's exactly the same as the beef they sell in the shops, young lady."

"How can it be, when it doesn't even come from a cow?" Matilda asks, certain her teenage logic can't be faulted. "It's just some chemical cocktail you've mixed up in your lab."

The cook wags her finger at Matilda. "Stop being melodramatic. I'll have you know every cell that goes into my beef patties is cloned from the highest quality Angus beef."

"Cloned… Yuk!" Matilda says, twisting her face into a snarl.

The cook grabs a spatula from a long rack of utensils and puts half a dozen juicy patties on the grill. A cloud of steam billows up. The cook waves her hand through the steam guiding it towards her face and inhales deeply. She turns to the three of you. "You smell that and tell me it's not as good as store-bought."

Instead of smelling the rich aroma, Matilda pinches her nose and turns away.

"It smells good, Matilda," you say, grabbing at her arm. "Just like barbecue at home."

Matilda turns and glares at you. "You wouldn't know a decent barbie if one burned you on the backside."

You and the apprentice exchange glances.

The apprentice leans toward you. "What's got into her?" he whispers into your ear.

"She's just hungry I think," you say. "But she doesn't like anything that isn't natural."

"Well that's just silly," the apprentice says. "Just because it's natural doesn't mean it's good for you. Take hemlock or arsenic or uranium or lead or…"

"Yeah, yeah, I get the idea," you say. "But try to convince her of that. Believe me I've tried."

You look around the strange restaurant. There's a small centrifuge at one end of the bench where most restaurants would have a coffee machine. "Do they do milkshakes?" you ask.

The apprentice shakes his head. "Only soy. They don't milk cows any more. Too bad for the environment with all the methane they fart out."

Matilda sighs. "It's like being on the set of some sci-fi movie. Why can't we just go somewhere that has normal food?"

"But it's 2040," the sorcerer says, "this is normal. There are nearly 9 billion people to feed."

The cook laughs at Matilda's expression when she hears this, and then walks towards the fridge. She pulls two Petri dishes off the top shelf and places them on the counter beside three dinner plates. Then using long-handled tweezers, she removes some green leaves off a bed of pink agar. "You lot want lettuce on your burgers don't you?" she asks.

Matilda groans in horror as the cook carefully lays a crispy green leaf on what looks to be a whole meal bun.

"Well I'm game," you say. "I'm so hungry I'd eat just about anything."

Matilda grunts. "I'd rather starve than eat tha—that Franken-food."

The cook laughs. "It's just lettuce silly girl. I've cloned it from real plants. In fact it's healthier than farm-grown because I know there aren't any pesticides on it. And, it's fresh."

"Yeah, Matilda," the sorcerer's apprentice says. "Lettuce is lettuce, however it's grown. They only use the purest growing agar here."

Matilda scrunches up her face. "You can't call something fresh just because you've plucked it out of some Petri dish that's been festering in the fridge. That makes no sense."

The cook ignores Matilda and raises her eyebrows at you. "NaCl?"

"What?" you ask."

"NaCl? Do you want some?'

The apprentice sits in silence, a smirk on his face.

"Yuck, chemicals," Matilda mutters under her breath as she glares at the cook. "Has the world gone mad?"

"NaCl is salt silly," the cook says. "Absolutely everything is made up of chemicals. Now, do you want a sprinkle of sodium chloride on your burger or not?"

Matilda sighs and looks up towards the ceiling. "I … want …a …real … burger!"

"These are real," the cook says. "Rare, medium or well done?"

"Medium for me," the apprentice says.

"Me too," you agree, "with onions and mustard if you've

got it."

As the patties finish cooking, the cook moves along the bench to the beaker bubbling away above the blue and yellow flame.

Slipping on a heat-proof glove she lifts the beaker, holds it in front of her face, and swirls its contents. Satisfied the correct consistency has been achieved, she turns back to face the three of you. "Cheese sauce? It's vintage cheddar."

"Are you nuts?" Matilda howls. "That's not cheese!"

"Its chemical composition is exactly 100% cheese," the cook says. "I should know, I brewed it up this morning."

While Matilda sticks her finger down her throat and pretends to gag, you hear your stomach rumble. "Yes please," you say. "I love cheddar."

"In fact," the cook says stepping up to Matilda, "if I gave you my formula and what you call 'real' cheese, you couldn't tell the difference."

"I bet I could!" Matilda says.

The cook pours a small amount of her mixture into a spoon and passes it to Matilda. "Go on then. Taste it. Give me your honest opinion."

Matilda is reluctant at first. Then with a sigh she takes the spoon and smells. "I got to admit it smells like cheese."

"Go on. Taste it." the cook says.

Matilda lifts the spoon to her lips, squeezes her eyes closed and puts the spoon in her mouth. "Hmmm…" she says. "That's not bad."

"See, I told you. As long as the chemical composition is

the same, cheese is cheese no matter how you make it."

The cook lifts the beaker back to her nose and sniffs. "Perfect."

A girl about your age comes into the restaurant. She has long green hair and bangs. "Is that barbequed bovine I smell?"

The cook smiles. 'I'm making burgers for our visitors,' she says. "Want one?"

"Yes please," the girl says. "You make the best burgers in the whole universe."

"They're not real burgers," Matilda grumps. "She's grown the meat in her lab."

The cook gives the girl a smile "Don't listen to her, she doesn't understand how cloning works. She's from the past, poor girl."

The cook holds up the salt shaker. "Would you like some NaCl on your burger?"

"Yes please," the girl says. "It makes everything taste so much better."

"Okay, but just a little. Everything in moderation."

Matilda is back to sticking her finger down her throat and making retching noises.

"Stop that!" you say. "You're embarrassing me. Besides, it's rude."

Matilda grumbles, but does as she's asked.

"Let's grab a seat by the window so we can admire the view," the apprentice says.

You waste no time moving over to a table that looks out

over the city. Through light smog, you see a number of high-rise complexes, elevated transport thoroughfares, and hydroponic garden towers. Beyond the buildings, you catch a glimpse of the yellow-grey harbor, a faint chemical haze rising from its surface.

The newcomer comes over to your table. She seems to know the apprentice. "Hi," she says, "mind if I join you?"

"Sure," the apprentice says, pointing towards an empty chair. "These are my new friends."

As the girl sweeps a lock of green hair behind her right ear, you stare mesmerized at the large brown eye in the centre of her forehead. The girl smiles at you, and is about to says something when she catches a glimpse of her reflection in the glass.

"Oh no," she says, touching a small lump on her eyelid. "I've got a sty coming on."

"Don't worry," the cook says, placing a tray of burgers on the table. "I've genetically engineered this batch of lettuce to have antibiotic properties. Any infection should clear up in no time."

Matilda looks down at the burgers like she expecting them to grow legs and walk off. "Ewww!" she says, turning up her nose.

"I'll tell you what, Matilda," the sorcerer's apprentice says. "If you two answer the next question correctly, you can have some ice cream. How's that?"

Afraid the apprentice might send you off somewhere before you've eaten, you grab a burger and take a bite.

"Mmmmmm," you say, chewing like crazy. "These are great."

The girl with the one eye grabs one too, as does the apprentice.

Matilda crosses her arms for a moment, but then her hunger gets the better of her and she takes a burger too. "At least if I grow an eye in the middle of my head, I'll know what to blame." She bites in.

The girl laughs. "Burgers didn't make me this way. I'm from the far side of the solar system. My family travelled though a worm hole and arrived here a few years ago. We've been helping you humans clean up the mess you made of your planet. We're due to go home next week."

"Wow!" you say. "I noticed you were a little different, but I didn't want to be rude."

Matilda swallows. "Jeez, and I though Australia was a long way away."

The next few minutes are passed in silence as then four of you gobble down your food.

After wiping the juice off his chin, the apprentice pulls a small piece of paper out of his pocket. "Okay here's the next one. You ready?"

With a full stomach, you're ready for anything. You nod. "Do your worst."

The apprentice starts to read. "Right. What country sent the first man into space? Now be careful, you could end up anywhere."

It's time to make a decision:

142

Which statement is correct?
The first man in space was from the China. **P143**
The first man in space was from the U.S.S.R. **P147**
The first man in space was from the U.S.A. **P196**

China

When the pink mist clears, the sorcerer's apprentice is shaking his head. "Oops. I really thought you'd get that last one right."

You look around and see that you've been transported to the top of a massive stone wall. The wall runs along a mountainous ridge in both directions for as far as you can see. Watchtowers dot the wall every few miles.

"Is this what I think it is?" you ask the apprentice.

The apprentice shrugs. "Maybe. What are you thinking?"

"Is this the great wall of China?"

"How do you know about the great wall?" the apprentice asks.

"School," you reply. "I was once told that the Great Wall of China was the only manmade structure that was visible from space with the naked eye."

The apprentice chuckles. "Well whoever told you that obviously wasn't an astronaut. That's a common myth.

Astronauts can see city lights at night, but the wall, despite its size, is just too small to see without magnification of some sort." The apprentice points up the ridge towards one of the towers built into the wall. "Still, it's an impressive sight don't you think?"

"Let's check it out," Matilda says, heading up a series of shallow stone steps. "I want to get a photo from the top of that tower."

You glance over at the apprentice. "Are we allowed?"

"Okay but be careful," the apprentice says, taking off after Matilda. "This part of the wall is unmanned at the moment, but there could be northern tribesmen about."

"Northern tribesmen?" you ask as you climb the steps. Then you see the smirk on the apprentice's face. "Have you taken us back in time again?"

He nods. "I was wondering when you'd notice the lack of tourists. We're back at the time of the Ming dynasty."

"Ming? Like the famous pottery?" you ask.

"Yep, that's the one. The Chinese made lots of advances in ceramic manufacture from 1368 to 1644. They used to export it all over the world."

"Just like today," you say. "Only now they make all sorts of stuff."

Your comment gives the apprentice pause for thought. "Yeah, I suppose you're right."

The two of you head off in pursuit of Matilda. When you finally reach the base of the watchtower you find her sitting on the parapet, a low wall that runs along each side of the wall's top, designed to give troops protection from invaders, and to stop traders and their pack animals from falling over the edge. From this position, the full extent of the wall can be seen as it runs up and over hill after hill.

"Wow, this wall is bigger than I ever imagined," you say

Matilda seems unimpressed. "I'm hungry," she says. "It must be all this fresh air and exercise. Can you snap up some fried rice?"

The apprentice ignores your Australian friend and continues his history lesson. "They used these towers to watch out for the Mongol hoards, and would light fires or send other signals if danger was spotted. After 200 years or so, by the time all the different sections were built and joined up, the wall was about 5500 miles long and had 25,000 watchtowers."

"Wow," you say. "That's like Los Angeles to New York."

"And back," the apprentice says. "LA to New York is only 2,400 miles."

"Crikey," Matilda says, "and to think they did it all by hand."

"Yep," the apprentice says, "millions of men over hundreds of years."

"This is all very interesting," you say, "but how are we going to get home from here?"

The apprentice reaches for his pocket. "How about I ask you another question. Maybe you'll get it right this time?"

You think a moment. "Okay," you say with a shrug. "What have I got to lose?"

146

The apprentice reads what's on the paper in front of him. "Here we go. What is the capital of China? If you get this right we'll go and have some ice cream.

You see Matilda's eyes light up.

"But if you get it wrong," the apprentice says, giving you a serious look. "I'll have to spin the dial on the time machine and who knows where we'll end up."

It is time to make a decision.

Is the capital of China:

Beijing? **P152**

Or

Tokyo? **P147**

Red Square

"Where are we now?" you ask, rubbing your temples as the mist clears. "This time travelling is giving me a headache."

Matilda hugs herself and shivers. "Well it's not tropical northern Australia. That's for sure."

"It's not Tokyo either," you say, looking around.

The sky is cloudy and the air is cold. You are standing in the middle of a huge cobblestoned plaza. The buildings around it are like nothing you've ever seen. Have you been transported into a fairytale?

The largest building has towering bricked walls topped with striped turrets shaped like upside-down onions. One turret has spiraling blue and white stripes. Another has a cross-hatch of red and green. One has stripes of green and gold — and there are more. The top turret looks like it's made from solid gold as it shimmers in the light.

You look around for the apprentice and find him standing behind you. He is wearing a long overcoat and a fur cap. "Welcome to Red Square," he says.

"Where's that?" Matilda asks.

"In Moscow," he says, "the capital of Russia. So what do you think of St. Basil's Cathedral?"

"The one with the turrets?" you ask.

The apprentice nods. "Beautiful isn't it."

"Why did you bring us here?" you ask. "Are you trying to get us arrested as spies by the KGB?"

The apprentice chuckles and shakes his head. "It's only 1861. The cathedral's just been completed. The KGB doesn't even exist yet."

"Jeez," Matilda says. "We'll never get home at this rate."

The apprentice ignores Matilda's whining. "A few apprentices have been Russian you know. One was even close to the royal family. Ever heard of Rasputin? He was a confidant of Nicholas II, the last tsar. "

"I've heard of Rasputin! Was he really a sorcerer's apprentice?" you ask.

"Not a very good one, unfortunately," the apprentice says. "He caused quite an uproar in his day."

"What did he do wrong?" Matilda asks.

"Rather than finishing the maze like he was supposed to, he decided to stop answering questions and become a wandering mystic. Broke all the rules. Got poor Nicholas in all sorts of trouble. But we don't have time for a Russian history lesson. You'll have to Google him when you get back home."

"If we get back," Matilda says, stomping her feet to stay warm. "Assuming I don't die from cold or hunger first!"

SNAP!

Suddenly you and Matilda are wearing fur hats and long coats like the apprentice.

Matilda smiles, "Great coat! Now, how about rustling up some ice cream?"

The apprentice frowns. "You never stop trying do you?"

"I didn't get where I am today without trying," she says, standing a little taller and looking rather pleased with herself.

"What are you talking about? You're in Russia!" you yell at her. "It's winter and it's freezing! You sent us back in time!" You shake your head in amazement. "…I didn't get where I am today… Jeez, Matilda, what's wrong with you?"

"Nothing a large bowl of ice cream wouldn't fix," she says, with a smirk. "Relax. The sorcerer's apprentice here has got everything under control."

"Grrrrr…" You turn away and stomp off across the square.

"Hey where are you going?" the apprentice yells out after you. "You need to answer the next question!"

"Rasputin didn't!" you say without turning around.

Let 'em sweat, you think. Surely the apprentice isn't allowed to lose you while you're in the maze. Maybe you'll go have a look at the cathedral.

SNAP!

You are instantly back beside the apprentice. "Stay put and do as you're told," he growls. "One Rasputin in history is enough. Now, answer this next question and you'll move closer to home."

"Or get ice cream," Matilda says glancing towards the apprentice. "That's a possibility too isn't it? I'm sure I heard you mention ice cream."

The apprentice sighs and stares back at Matilda. "If I say having ice cream is a possibility will you shut up for a few minutes?"

Matilda mimes zipping her mouth shut.

"Okay…" the apprentice says reluctantly. "It's a possibility … a faint one. Happy now?"

Matilda smiles, and then turns to you. "See? I told ya that Persistence is my middle name."

"But get the question wrong and I'll send you further back," the apprentice says. "Would you like that? Miss Persistence?"

"Like a poke in the eye with a burnt stick," Matilda says.

"Translation?" the apprentice says, turning to you.

"She wouldn't be happy."

The apprentice scratches his head. "Right, hmmm…"

Matilda stomps her foot. "Well don't keep us in suspenders, Mister apprentice. Read out the question. I'm starving in case you'd forgotten."

"Matilda! Stop being a pain in the butt," you say.

"No pain, no gain," she replies.

"I don't think that's what that saying means," you say.

"It does in Australia," she insists. "When I'm a pain, I get gain."

"No wonder they sent you overseas to school," you say, before turning towards the apprentice. "You may as well get it over with, but please don't ask me about Russia. All I know about Russia is that it's the largest country in the world. Followed by Canada and the United States."

The apprentice nods and reaches for his pocket. "Ah... Here's a good one. You should get this."

"You'd better!" Matilda says glaring at you for a moment. Then she smiles. "Just joking. No pressure."

"Right," the apprentice says. "What is the most accurate clock in the world? Is it:"

A grandfather clock? **P181**

Or

An atomic clock? **P186**

Welcome to the sorcerer's ice cream parlor

When the mist clears, you find yourself in a large ice cream parlor with a long counter and lots of tables. The place echoes with groups eating and laughing. The apprentice is dressed like a clown in a bright blue jumpsuit with yellow dots and floppy red shoes.

"Well done. Time for ice cream," he says, with a grin.

"Yippee!" Matilda cries. "Nom, nom, nom!"

The apprentice taps one of his over-sized shoes on the floor. "Okay, what's your favorite flavor? Quick now, before the sorcerer changes his mind."

"Kangaroo," Matilda says with a laugh. "Skippy if you've got it."

The sorcerer's apprentice gives Matilda a confused looked. "I—I'm not sure the sorcerer does kangaroo ice—"

"Ha! Gottcha!" Matilda shouts. "Jeez mate, for a sorcerer's apprentice you're awfully gullible. Nah, seriously, I'll have passion fruit if you've got it."

The apprentice swivels around. "And you?"

"Chocolate, please." you say, "with chocolate chips, chocolate sprinkles and chocolate sauce."

"Right," the apprentice says. "One kangaroo and one vanilla coming up."

As the apprentice goes to the counter, you and Matilda find a seat.

"I wonder who all these people are?" Matilda asks. "Do you reckon they're on trips through the maze too?"

You study the groups. "They could be. Did you notice every table has one person dressed like a clown?

Matilda scans the room. "You're right, there's a whole circus of them."

"Here we go," the sorcerer's apprentice says placing a bowl in front of each of you. "Now eat."

"Strewth mate! What the bleedin' heck you call this? There's hair and—and, all sorts of stuff in mine."

"Who the gullible one now?" the apprentice says, giving Matilda a wink. "You really think the sorcerer can't make kangaroo ice cream?"

"Ewww," Matilda says, shoving the bowl away. "I need this like a submarine needs a screen door."

"Translation?" the apprentice says, looking at you.

"She's not happy," you say with a chuckle.

Matilda harrumphs. "Would you be? Jeez, bloke can't

even take a joke."

The apprentice takes a bite of his ice cream and lets Matilda stew. Then, he snaps his fingers over her bowl, and in a puff of sweet-smelling smoke, her kangaroo ice cream transforms into passion fruit, topped with a juicy pulp filled with tiny black seeds.

"Now that's more like it!" Matilda shouts. She grabs a spoon and digs in. "Neat trick."

"The sorcerer teaches all of his apprentices magic. You'd be surprised what I can do."

Matilda swallows a big mouthful. "How did you become an apprentice?"

"Anyone can do it. I'll tell you at the end of the maze. If you get there," he says. "In the meantime, finish your ice cream. You've got more questions to answer."

"So are all these clowns apprentices?" you ask.

The boy nods as he shovels ice cream into his mouth.

You do some quick calculations. "But there must be 50 of them."

The boy swallows. "The sorcerer needs lot of apprentices to show visitors through his mazes and to help with all the questions. Your next question was made up by a boy named Luke."

You and Matilda scoop up the last of your ice cream as the apprentice pulls a piece of paper out of his pocket. "Okay, here we go. Get this right and we'll go someplace fun. Get it wrong and you might wish you were wearing something warmer."

"You're not going to stuff us in the freezer with the ice cream are you?" Matilda asks.

The apprentice shakes his head. "Not quite," he says. "Right, here's your question. At what temperature is Fahrenheit and Celsius the same?"

It is time for your decision.

Is it:

Zero degrees? **P156**

Or

Minus 40 degrees? **P160**

156

You have chosen zero degrees

"Oops, that's not right," the sorcerer's apprentice says. "Looks like I'll have to spin the dial and see where we end up. Hold on!"

FLASH—BANG!

This time the mist is blue and cold. As it clears, the freezing cloud sinks to the ground, but doesn't disappear altogether. When you look around, you find yourself standing on the bank of a river. The water rushing past is light blue in color because of the flecks of ice suspended in it. Further upstream, about half a mile or so, is a huge wall of ice with pointed pinnacles. Icebergs float in the water at the foot of the ice.

A bitter wind blows down the valley, rustling your hair and chilling your ears. Goose bumps pop up on your arm.

"Whoa!" Matilda says. "Is that a glacier up there?"

"Good guess," the sorcerer's apprentice says.

"It's free—freezing," you say between chattering teeth. "Any cha—chance of a quick question before I get hypothermia?"

The apprentice snaps his fingers and a long hairy robe appears over your shoulders. It smells a bit rank, but it cuts the wind and stops your teeth from chattering. Matilda has been transformed into a cave girl in her roughly-fashioned wrap.

You pluck at your garment. "By the looks of the clothing you've given us, I'm guessing we've gone back in time again?"

"Well spotted," the apprentice says. "We've gone back to the last ice age 14,000 years ago."

But Matilda isn't listening. Her face is screwed into an expression of disgust as she picks at something in her coat "This thing smells like wombat pee," she complains, pinching her nose between her thumb and forefinger. "If it weren't so cold…"

"They cured animal skins with urine back then," the apprentice says. "Pee's got ammonia in it. Sorry if you're not happy."

"Too right I'm not happy," Matilda says. "It's got fleas too."

The apprentice snaps his finger and dozens of small insects fall like pepper onto the snow at Matilda's feet. "There you go," he says, "no more fleas."

"But the smell…" she says.

SNAP! A strawberry cloud surrounds Matilda.

"Now, can we get on with it?" the apprentice says, giving Matilda a sharp look.

"Yeah, thanks," Matilda says. She licks her lips. "That's much better."

"So what's next?" you ask. "Are you going to question us about the Ice Age?"

The apprentice is about to answer when a sharp crack breaks the silence. Further up the valley, a pillar of the ice the size of a 10 story building shears off the glacier. With a huge splash, the ice crashes into the water at the glacier's base. A thirty-foot wave rushes down the river towards you.

"Quick! Get to higher ground!" the apprentice shouts, before turning and running up the slope.

You quickly follow as the wave roars down the valley picking up rocks and other debris as it goes. Matilda is right beside you pumping her arms furiously as she rushes up the hill.

"Up here," the apprentice says, scrambling up a gravel slope between two huge boulders.

You don't need to look back to tell the wave is closing. The rumbling is right behind you. Just as you reach the top, the water rushes past, only yards below.

You lie on the ground, panting.

"Crikey, tha—that was close!" Matilda says, gasping for air. "Thought we were goners."

Your hands are shaking, and it's not from the cold. "Can

we leave now?" you ask the apprentice. "Getting killed wasn't on my 'to do' list today.

"Good idea," he says, pulling a piece of paper from his pocket. "The sorcerer would be pretty annoyed if I lost you mid-maze." He tucks the time machine under his arm and reads from the paper. "The glaciers are shrinking. In fact we're standing on a pile of rock that the glacier pushed down the mountain before it retreated. What is this pile of rock called?"

"I think I know this one!" Matilda says. "Please can I answer it?"

But you think you know the answer too. What should you do?

It is time to make your next decision. Is the pile of rock called:

A glacial moraine? **P165**

Or

A glacial meringue? **P188**

Or

Do you let Matilda answer the question? **P186**

160

You have chosen minus 40 degrees

"Well done," the apprentice says.

You give him a smile. "Yeah, well I knew that 0 degrees was freezing in Celsius and 32 was freezing in Fahrenheit so it had to be the other choice."

"Nice logic," the apprentice says. "You used what is known as 'the process of elimination' to work it out. You eliminated a wrong answer and it left you with the correct one."

"Whatever," Matilda says with a sigh. "Are you going to get us closer to home, or are you two going to stand around and chinwag all day?"

"Be patient," the apprentice says. "I just need to decide where I should take you."

"Somewhere warm," you suggest. "All this talk of freezing has made me nervous."

The apprentice scratches his head, then smiles. "I have an idea..." He holds up the box and turns the dial.

You stick your fingers in your ears. The coil glows red. The air crackles.

FLASH–BANG!

"Crikey that was loud," Matilda says as the mist clears. "My ears are ringing."

White sand and coconut palms edge a crystal clear ocean like pictures you've seen on postcards. The water is calm, with barely a ripple on its surface. Gulls dip and dive.

The apprentice is submerged up to his chest. "Come on

in," he yells, "the water's fantastic!"

The sun blazes down. Grains of sand squeak between your toes. You certainly got your wish for somewhere warm.

"Last one in is a wombat's bum!" Matilda shrieks as she dashes for the sea.

You take off after her. By the time she reaches the water's edge, the two of you are side by side. You plough through the shallows until the water is thigh deep then plunge forward arching into a shallow dive. But when you surface and look around, the apprentice is nowhere to be seen.

"Where'd he go?" Matilda says, searching for the boy. "I hope that cheeky sod hasn't deserted us."

"He's probably diving for shells. He wouldn't leave without us would he?"

"Blowed if I know, mate."

"Well I'm going for a swim," you say before paddling out a little further. "Look how clear the water is."

Then your stomach lurches. A grey fin is cutting though the water further out. "Umm… Matilda…" You raise an arm and point at the triangle as it turns in a gentle arc, heading closer. "Is that what I think it is?"

"Bleedin' heck!" Matilda says. She turns and thrashes her way towards the shore. "I'm not sure what it is," she says over her shoulder, "but I'm not hangin' round to find out."

A second fin pops out of the water, and a third. Before you've had a chance to react, they streak towards you. A shadow moves under the water right beside you.

"Ahhhhhhhhhhh!" you scream.

162

When the apprentice surfaces, there is a huge grin on his face. "Fancy a dolphin ride?" he says. "Oh, sorry… Did I give you a fright?"

"Give me a fright!" you shout. "I thought you were a shark! I nearly pooped myself!"

You hear cackling from the beach. When you turn towards shore, Matilda is standing in ankle-deep water, clutching at her sides, laughing.

"You should have seen your face." she says, pointing at you. "I didn't realize human eyes could bug out like that."

"Sorry," the boy said. "I thought you knew the difference between dolphins and sharks."

"Obviously not!" you snap, wishing your heart would stop banging so hard in your chest.

"Well for future reference, the back of a sharks fin is pretty straight up and down. Dolphin dorsal fins are more curved."

"Might pay to tell that to your guests a little earlier next time," you say. "Save on laundry."

But your fright goes away when the dolphins surface beside the boy. They have smiley faces and sparkling eyes. He strokes one of the dolphins under its chin.

Another rubs its narrow snout against your arm to get your attention.

"I think they want to play," the apprentice says. He lifts one leg over a dolphin's back and grabbing gently onto its dorsal fin. "Climb on. It's like riding a horse, only wetter."

A dolphin nudges you again, so you do as the apprentice

suggests and climb on.

The dolphin's skin is smooth and has a slightly rubbery texture to it, almost like the creature is wearing a wet suit. Sitting on its back, you feel warmth radiate from its body. The dolphin makes a series of squeaky clicks then starts to swim after the apprentice.

"Oi! Wait for me you lot!" Matilda yells, splashing back into the water. "Here dolphin, come to Matilda."

As if understanding her words, the last dolphin streaks over to Matilda and allows her to climb onto its back.

"Where are they taking us?" you ask the apprentice as the dolphins move into formation, three abreast. You point to a speck of land in the distance. "Are we going to that island?"

The island looks to be about a mile offshore. It's small and only has a few palm trees on it.

"We're going to visit the sea turtles," the apprentice says. "The island is part of Ulithi atoll, one of their most important nesting sites."

The dolphins' tails are powerful as they move up and down, propelling the three of you though the water. As you near the beach, the water becomes shallower and bright corals and schools of small, colorful fish appear beneath you.

The sea around you is busy with life. Urchins, anemones, starfish and crabs clutter the bottom, while fish swim in groups. They jink left, then right, searching for food amongst the coral and avoiding the larger fish who'd like them for lunch.

164

Then you see your first turtle. Its carapace, or shell, is a brownish-green and is at least a yard wide.

"Wow they're so big!" you say. "I expected them to be smaller."

"Adults can grow to over 600 pounds," the apprentice says.

"That's a lot of turtle soup," Matilda says. "Not that I'm suggesting—"

"—you'd better not be," the apprentice says a little sharply, "they're endangered. Now, the next question is about turtles, so listen carefully." The apprentice climbs off his dolphin and walks up onto the beach.

You and Matilda follow.

"Mother turtles crawl up the beach and dig a hole in the sand with their back flippers," the apprentice says. "Then they lay their eggs before covering them up. After two months, when the baby turtles hatch, they're only a couple of inches long."

"How many eggs do they lay?" you ask.

"Ah… I see you've stumbled upon my next question. How many eggs *do* they lay? Now if you get this right, you'll nearly be home. But if you get this one wrong, I'll have to send you back in time. So, which statement is correct?"

Green sea turtles lay between 10 and 20 eggs in each nest. **P181**

Or

Green sea turtles lay between 100 and 200 eggs in each nest. **P186**

You have been sent to the future

"Surprise!" the sorcerer's apprentice says. "Welcome to the future."

When the pink mist clears, you find yourself sitting at a long counter in a strange restaurant. Behind the counter, a stainless steel bench runs the length of the wall. In its centre is a gas grill. Beside the grill, a glass beaker filled with thick orange liquid bubbles in a Bunsen burner. The rest of the bench is covered in racks of test tubes, numerous glass beakers, funnels, and other equipment.

"They do good burgers here in 2040," the apprentice says. "The beef is grown in the lab. Very tender."

Matilda frowns. "But I don't want a hamburger grown in some Petri dish. That sounds gross!"

The cook behind the counter shakes her head and wipes

her hands on her apron. "It's exactly the same as the beef they sell in the shops, young lady."

"How can it be, when it doesn't even come from a cow?" Matilda asks, certain her teenage logic can't be faulted. "It's just some chemical cocktail you've mixed up in your lab."

The cook wags her finger at Matilda. "Stop being melodramatic. I'll have you know every cell that goes into my beef patties is cloned from the highest quality Angus beef."

"Cloned… Yuk!" Matilda says, twisting her face into a snarl.

The cook grabs a spatula from a long rack of utensils and puts half a dozen juicy patties on the grill. A cloud of steam billows up. The cook waves her hand through the steam guiding it towards her face and inhales deeply. She turns to the three of you. "You smell that and tell me it's not as good as store-bought."

Instead of smelling the rich aroma, Matilda pinches her nose and turns away.

"It smells good, Matilda," you say, grabbing at her arm. "Just like barbecue at home."

Matilda turns and glares at you. "You wouldn't know a decent barbie if one burned you on the backside."

You and the apprentice exchange glances.

The apprentice leans toward you. "What's got into her?" he whispers into your ear.

"She's just hungry I think," you say. "But she doesn't like anything that isn't natural."

"Well that's just silly," the apprentice says. "Just because it's natural doesn't mean it's good for you. Take hemlock or arsenic or uranium or lead or…"

"Yeah, yeah, I get the idea," you say. "But try to convince her of that. Believe me I've tried."

You look around the strange restaurant. There's a small centrifuge at one end of the bench where most restaurants would have a coffee machine. "Do they do milkshakes?" you ask.

The apprentice shakes his head. "Only soy. They don't milk cows any more. Too bad for the environment with all the methane they fart out."

Matilda sighs. "It's like being on the set of some sci-fi movie. Why can't we just go somewhere that has normal food?"

"But it's 2040," the sorcerer says, "this is normal. There are nearly 9 billion people to feed."

The cook laughs at Matilda's expression when she hears this, and then walks towards the fridge. She pulls two Petri dishes off the top shelf and places them on the counter beside three dinner plates. Then using long-handled tweezers, she removes some green leaves off a bed of pink agar. "You lot want lettuce on your burgers don't you?" she asks.

Matilda groans in horror as the cook carefully lays a crispy green leaf on what looks to be a whole meal bun.

"Well I'm game," you say. "I'm so hungry I'd eat just about anything."

Matilda grunts. "I'd rather starve than eat tha—that Franken-food."

The cook laughs. "It's just lettuce silly girl. I've cloned it from real plants. In fact it's healthier than farm-grown because I know there aren't any pesticides on it. And, it's fresh."

"Yeah, Matilda," the sorcerer's apprentice says. "Lettuce is lettuce, however it's grown. They only use the purest growing agar here."

Matilda scrunches up her face. "You can't call something fresh just because you've plucked it out of some Petri dish that's been festering in the fridge. That makes no sense."

The cook ignores Matilda and raises her eyebrows at you. "NaCl?"

"What?" you ask."

"NaCl? Do you want some?'

The apprentice sits in silence, a smirk on his face.

"Yuck, chemicals," Matilda mutters under her breath as she glares at the cook. "Has the world gone mad?"

"NaCl is salt silly," the cook says. "Absolutely everything is made up of chemicals. Now, do you want a sprinkle of sodium chloride on your burger or not?"

Matilda sighs and looks up towards the ceiling. "I … want …a …real … burger!"

"These are real," the cook says. "Rare, medium or well done?"

"Medium for me," the apprentice says.

"Me too," you agree, "with onions and mustard if you've

got it."

As the patties finish cooking, the cook moves along the bench to the beaker bubbling away above the blue and yellow flame.

Slipping on a heat-proof glove she lifts the beaker, holds it in front of her face, and swirls its contents. Satisfied the correct consistency has been achieved, she turns back to face the three of you. "Cheese sauce? It's vintage cheddar."

"Are you nuts?" Matilda howls. "That's not cheese!"

"Its chemical composition is exactly 100% cheese," the cook says. "I should know, I brewed it up this morning."

While Matilda sticks her finger down her throat and pretends to gag, you hear your stomach rumble. "Yes please," you say. "I love cheddar."

"In fact," the cook says stepping up to Matilda, "if I gave you my formula and what you call 'real' cheese, you couldn't tell the difference."

"I bet I could!" Matilda says.

The cook pours a small amount of her mixture into a spoon and passes it to Matilda. "Go on then. Taste it. Give me your honest opinion."

Matilda is reluctant at first. Then with a sigh she takes the spoon and smells. "I got to admit it smells like cheese."

"Go on. Taste it." the cook says.

Matilda lifts the spoon to her lips, squeezes her eyes closed and puts the spoon in her mouth. "Hmmm…" she says. "That's not bad."

"See, I told you. As long as the chemical composition is

the same, cheese is cheese no matter how you make it."

The cook lifts the beaker back to her nose and sniffs. "Perfect."

A girl about your age comes into the restaurant. She has long green hair and bangs. "Is that barbequed bovine I smell?"

The cook smiles. 'I'm making burgers for our visitors,' she says. "Want one?"

"Yes please," the girl says. "You make the best burgers in the whole universe."

"They're not real burgers," Matilda grumps. "She's grown the meat in her lab."

The cook gives the girl a smile "Don't listen to her, she doesn't understand how cloning works. She's from the past, poor girl."

The cook holds up the salt shaker. "Would you like some NaCl on your burger?"

"Yes please," the girl says. "It makes everything taste so much better."

"Okay, but just a little. Everything in moderation."

Matilda is back to sticking her finger down her throat and making retching noises.

"Stop that!" you say. "You're embarrassing me. Besides, it's rude."

Matilda grumbles, but does as she's asked.

"Let's grab a seat by the window so we can admire the view," the apprentice says.

You waste no time moving over to a table that looks out

over the city. Through light smog, you see a number of high-rise complexes, elevated transport thoroughfares, and hydroponic garden towers. Beyond the buildings, you catch a glimpse of the yellow-grey harbor, a faint chemical haze rising from its surface.

The newcomer comes over to your table. She seems to know the apprentice. "Hi," she says, "mind if I join you?"

"Sure," the apprentice says, pointing towards an empty chair. "These are my new friends."

As the girl sweeps a lock of green hair behind her right ear, you stare mesmerized at the large brown eye in the centre of her forehead. The girl smiles at you, and is about to says something when she catches a glimpse of her reflection in the glass.

"Oh no," she says, touching a small lump on her eyelid. "I've got a sty coming on."

"Don't worry," the cook says, placing a tray of burgers on the table. "I've genetically engineered this batch of lettuce to have antibiotic properties. Any infection should clear up in no time."

Matilda looks down at the burgers like she expecting them to grow legs and walk off. "Ewww!" she says, turning up her nose.

"I'll tell you what, Matilda," the sorcerer's apprentice says. "If you two answer the next question correctly, you can have some ice cream. How's that?"

Afraid the apprentice might send you off somewhere before you've eaten, you grab a burger and take a bite.

"Mmmmmm," you say, chewing like crazy. "These are great."

The girl with the one eye grabs one too, as does the apprentice.

Matilda crosses her arms for a moment, but then her hunger gets the better of her and she takes a burger too. "At least if I grow an eye in the middle of my head, I'll know what to blame." She bites in.

The girl laughs. "Burgers didn't make me this way. I'm from the far side of the solar system. My family travelled though a worm hole and arrived here a few years ago. We've been helping you humans clean up the mess you made of your planet. We're due to go home next week."

"Wow!" you say. "I noticed you were a little different, but I didn't want to be rude."

Matilda swallows. "Jeez, and I though Australia was a long way away."

The next few minutes are passed in silence as then four of you gobble down your food.

After wiping the juice off his chin, the apprentice pulls a small piece of paper out of his pocket. "Okay here's the next one. You ready?"

With a full stomach, you're ready for anything. You nod. "Do your worst."

The apprentice starts to read. "Right. What country sent the first man into space? Now be careful, because one of these answers will send you back to the very beginning of the maze."

It's time to make a decision:
Which statement is correct?
The first man in space was from China. **P143**
The first man in space was from the U.S.S.R. **P147**
The first man in space was from the U.S.A. **P191**

174

Glacial moraine

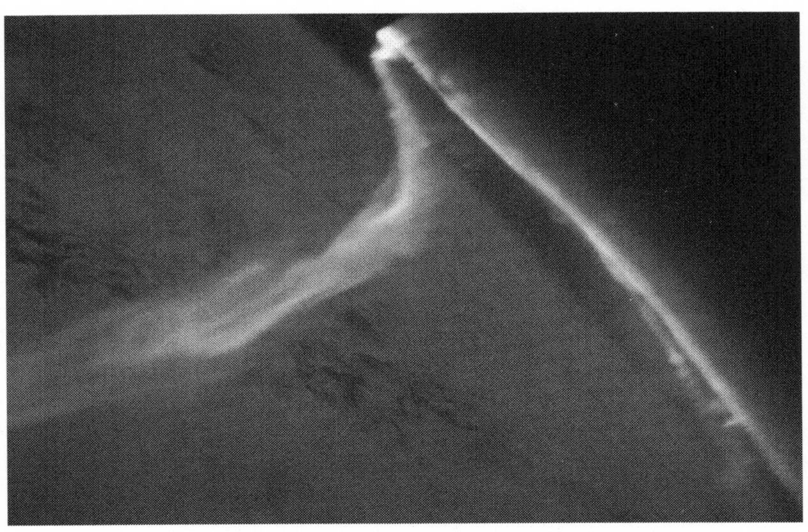

FLASH—BANG!

"That's righttttttttttttt," the apprentice says, his voice fading away.

You are falling down an endless tunnel. Colors swirl and static crackles all around you. What's going on? This isn't what usually happens when you travel through space-time. Have you fallen into a worm hole? Are you being sucked into an alternative universe? Did Matilda cause this somehow?

You grit your teeth and squint to protect your eyes from the bursts of bright green, vivid blues, purples and hot pink light that twists and dances before you. It is all so strange.

Matilda streaks past you in a swirl of color. "Crikeyyyyyyyyyyyy!"

Where is she going? What is going on? "Matilda!" you yell.

Then, as fast as your falling started, you find yourself hovering above the horizon. The curve of the earth stretches out before you. Green lights flash and spread out. Waves dance and swirl, constantly changing as they flicker like flames across the sky.

"Streuth! That was different."

You turn to find Matilda floating beside you in a white space suit. The helmet's faceplate is made from clear plastic and you can see her startled expression clearly through it. In all the excitement, you hadn't noticed that you have a suit on too.

"What do you think of the aurora borealis?" say the apprentice.

You look around but he is nowhere to be seen.

"Beautiful isn't it?" the apprentice says.

His voice is coming directly into your helmet. Then you see him in the distance. He's floating towards you, adjusting his course as he does so with tiny jets of compressed air shooting from the pack attached to his back.

"What's going on? For a moment I thought we were falling through a worm hole." you say, looking down at the dancing lights.

The apprentice shakes his helmet. "Not quite. Pretty amazing show, don't you think?"

"What causes all the lights?" you ask.

"It happens when charged particles from the sun hit

electrons in our atmosphere."

As you watch the lights dance, your mind is taken off the fact that you're floating in space.

"I think I'm more worried about getting back to earth in one piece," Matilda says, breaking the spell "Haven't you forgotten something?"

The apprentice does a quick scan of the area, then looks back at Matilda. "Not that I can see…"

Matilda sighs in frustration and glares at the boy. "Like a bleedin' spaceship, you great galah!"

"Oh that," the apprentice chuckles. "Don't worry. I have a plan." He pulls the black box from a pouch on his right leg and starts fiddling with the dial. "Right, I've adjusted the time slightly, the space taxi should be along at any moment."

"Space taxi?" you say. "Are you serious?"

"Well, officially its call the International Space Station, but we should be able to cadge a lift if we ask nicely."

"Ha!" Matilda scoffs. "Ask nicely? That's your plan?"

"Seems to work for most things I've found," the apprentice says. "Oh here it comes, right on schedule. Clip on to my tether, I'll maneuver us over."

After you and Matilda are attached, the apprentice gives his jets a couple of long bursts so you match speed with the space station. Then with one final burst he brings you alongside the glistening craft.

"Grab hold and don't let go," the apprentice says, grabbing a handrail. "I'll send them a message and get them to open the air lock."

Matilda taps you on the shoulder. "I hope this wombat knows what he's doing."

"I can hear you Matilda!" the apprentice says. "ISS, this is the sorcerer's apprentice, we're just outside. Can we come aboard please?"

"This is the ISS. Please make your way to the airlock."

"Come on you two," the apprentice says, "time to make our grand entry."

The three of you work your way along the handrail to a door built into the side of the space station.

"Airlock, disengaged," a voice says in your helmet.

And with that, the door pops open, exposing an area the size of an elevator.

"Right, in we get," the apprentices says.

Once the three of you are inside, the apprentice pushes a button on the wall and the door closes with a hiss. A dial starts to move from red to green as the atmosphere inside the airlock is equalized with the main ship.

"Okay we can take off our suits now," the apprentice says. The inner door opens revealing a man wearing blue overalls. "Here let me help you with those."

The apprentice grins. "What do you think? Quite a place eh?"

Once the suits are stowed in lockers, the man leads you down a narrow corridor lined with pipes and other equipment. Everywhere you look are dials and ducts and wiring and control panels. Once through the corridor the space opens out, but it is still cluttered with equipment, microscopes, and other electronics. There are also three more people waiting to meet you, a man and a woman, also wearing blue, and a man with a Chinese flag on his suit.

The man in blue floats over to you and gives you all a puzzled look. "This is the first time we've picked up hitchhikers. I'm the captain of this mission. Do you mind telling me how the heck you got here?"

The apprentice smiles. "I'm guiding my friends through a space-time maze." He pulls out the black box. "Neat gadget, eh?"

The captain's face creases in confusion. "You got here with that—that box? But that's—"

"—impossible?" The apprentice shrugs. "How do you explain us being here then?"

The captain continues. "Hmmmm. Yes you have a point… So, how does it work?"

The apprentice smiles. "Well if I knew that, I'd be the sorcerer and not his apprentice, wouldn't I?"

"The sorcerer?" the captain says. "You mean you got here by magic?"

The apprentice nods. "If you call this box magic, then I guess we did. The sorcerer is a scientist that works at the Timescale Research Facility. This is his invention. I'm just running some field trials for him. It only seems like magic to those of us who can't explain it. To the sorcerer it's no more complicated than a microwave oven or a cell phone."

"Field trials? And you ended up here on the International Space Station? I'll have to contact Houston. They're going to flip when they hear about this."

The sorcerer's apprentice snaps his fingers.

FLASH—BANG!

The room filled with pink mist. When the mist clears you are sitting in a quiet waiting room. Matilda is to your right. You turn and face the apprentice. "What was that all about? And where are we now? Are we back on earth?"

"Yes, we had to go. Those astronauts were getting a bit nosey. So I brought us back to the sorcerer's place."

"But won't they want to know where we've gone?"

The apprentice grins. "Don't worry they won't remember a thing. The mist I left behind will see to that."

"You've given them amnesia?" Matilda says.

"I had to. We can't have people reporting they've seen time travelers. The authorities will think they're crazy and lock them up. That wouldn't be very nice of us now would it?"

Matilda laughs. "You're full of tricks aren't you?"

"Yep," the apprentice says. "That's what being a sorcerer's apprentice is all about."

"So this is the sorcerer's place?" you ask.

"Well actually it's the sorcerer's waiting room," the apprentice says. "Wait here, I'll go into his office and see if he's ready to see you yet."

With that, the boy snaps his fingers and disappears.

You give Matilda a look. "I wonder if this is the end of the maze then."

"Let's hope so," she says. "I'm famished."

180

A few minutes later, a booming voice comes over the intercom.

"It is time for another question," the voice rumbles.

"Crikey, that must be the sorcerer," Matilda says.

"If you get the question right, you will get to return home," the voice continues. "But if you get it wrong, I will send you back in time. So listen carefully."

"Which of the following statements is correct?"

The International Space Station orbits the earth every 90 minutes. **P186**

Or

The International Space Station orbits the earth once a day. **P181**

Back in time

"It's dark," Matilda says. "Where are we?"

"I think we're in a cave," you reply.

Standing quietly as your eyes adjust, you listen to the sounds around you. Somewhere further into the cave you hear the steady *plonk, plonk, plonk* of water dripping.

After a minute or so, you start to see shadows. A small amount of light is seeping into the cave through a crack high in the rock above you. Wisps of smoke drift up from the remnants of a fire inside a semicircle of rocks built up against one wall.

"Someone's been down here," you say. "And they haven't been gone very long by the looks of those ashes."

"Where's the apprentice?" Matilda asks, looking around nervously. "I hope he's not too far, it's chilly down here and

I'm a bit claustrophobic."

Next to the makeshift fireplace is a pile of branches. You kneel down on the ground and blow on the embers. A couple pieces glow red.

"I'll see if I can get this fire going," you say. "It'll warm us up and give us some light while we figure out what to do."

You grab one of the smaller branches and break it into pieces. These you lay gently over the embers.

"Don't smother it, mate," Matilda says. "It needs air to burn."

You purse you lips and blow. The extra oxygen makes the embers glow red-hot and before you know it, the small pile of kindling bursts into flames. Slowly, you add more twigs and branches to the growing fire.

It isn't until you look up from your task that you spot the paintings on the wall behind you.

"Whoa!" you say taking in the scene. "Matilda, look behind you!"

Matilda turns. Her eyes widen. "That's amazing!"

Matilda isn't exaggerating. The back wall of the cave, opposite the fire, is covered in simple, yet beautiful paintings. Images of deer, horses and other grazing animals stretch from one side of the cave to the other. One animal looks a bit like a giraffe. In the centre of the wall is a painting of a fire, not unlike your own. Around it, the artist has captured men, women and children dancing.

"These paintings must be really old," Matilda says, "but the colors are so bright. I've seen cave paintings in Australia similar to this, but they're always much fainter."

Then, past the picture of the people dancing, towards the far end of the wall, you see a picture of the apprentice. He is with two other people. Your mouth drops open and your hand slowly rises to point at the image. "Matilda, look! It's—it's us! The clothes are the same and the hair color, and the…"

You can see a full circle of white around Matilda's pupils when she sees the part of the painting you're indicating.

"Bleedin' heck! How is that possible?"

"I thought I'd arrive a little earlier and record our visit," a voice from the darkness says. The apprentice steps into the light. "I see you got the fire going."

"You painted that?" you ask. "But when?"

The apprentice laughs. "You don't understand space-time very well do you? I just set the sorcerer's time machine to drop me off an hour earlier so I could paint in peace before you two arrived."

"Well it's a good likeness, I'll give you that," Matilda says. "But I bet you confuse the anthropologists if they ever find this place."

"Oh well, nothing like a few mysteries to keep people guessing. I drew a spaceman in the last cave I visited, that'll really get them going."

"So where are we?" you ask.

"And what year is it?" Matilda asks.

"This is a cave in France. It will be found in about 17,000 years."

"17,000 years!" Matilda cries. "How are we going to get home from here?"

"Don't worry. Answer this next question right, and you'll be nearly home."

You shoot the apprentice a suspicious look. "You said that last time."

"It's true," the apprentice says. "You just have to get the answer right, that's all."

You kick the ground. "Okay, but how about something easy for a change?"

"I'll see what I can do. If I give you an easy question, and you get it wrong, I'll have to send you all the way back to the beginning of the maze. You sure you want that?"

"All the way back?" you ask.

"That's not a fair suck of the sav," Matilda says.

The apprentice looks confused and turns toward you. "Translation?" he says.

"It's unfair. She doesn't like it," you say.

"Sorry, Matilda. I don't make the rules," the apprentice says.

You turn and face Matilda. "What do you think? Should we go for an easy one?"

"Give it a go, mate. We're 17,000 years from home. How much worse could it get?"

You glance at the apprentice. "You did say easy didn't you?"

"Yes but 'easy' is a relative term. For a monkey, climbing a tree is easy, but for an elephant … not so much." The apprentice gives you a smile. "So, are you a monkey or an elephant?"

You're not really sure what monkeys and elephants have to do with this decision, but you do like climbing trees. Maybe that's a clue. You scratch your head and think a moment.

"Come on ya galah. Go for it." Matilda urges.

"Okay," you say to the apprentice. "We'll go for it."

"Right … here we go. This cave painting is in France. But where is France?"

Is France in South America? **P191**

Or

Is France in Europe? **P186**

Nearly home

"Well done," the apprentice says once the mist has cleared. "You've only got one more question to answer correctly and you get to go home."

"It's about time," Matilda says. "I'm so peckish I could eat the foot off a low flying duck."

The apprentice looks at you with a confused expression on his face. "Translation?"

"She's very, very hungry," you say, shaking your head. "Don't worry, you get used to it after a while."

Ignoring Matilda, you scan the countryside. Gently rolling hills covered with green grass and sheep rise off into the distance. A few craggy old trees dot the ridgeline.

You glance over at the apprentice. "Where are we? And where did all these sheep come from?"

"Ah ha," the apprentice says. "That is a very good question."

"If I figure it out, will we get to go home?" you ask

"At least there's lots to eat if we get stuck," Matilda says eying up the nearest sheep. "Baaaaa!" she bleats. "Baaaaaaa!"

The sheep glances up from its grassy meal, takes one look at Matilda, and races off to join the rest of the flock.

"Go on, run!" Matilda yells after the startled beast. "But remember, I know where you live!"

"Do you always have that effect on sheep, Matilda?" you ask, trying not to laugh.

"Sheep and young children," Matilda answers with a

straight face.

The apprentice covers his mouth to stifle a laugh. “Ahem… So, are you ready for your last question?”

You nod. “Ready as I’ll ever be I guess.”

The apprentice reaches into his pocket and pulls out a piece of paper. “Right here are a few hints. All you’ve got to do it tell me which country we’re in. But be careful. Get it wrong and I’ll have to spin the dial and send you off to who knows where.”

He hands you the paper.

Hint one: This country has the southernmost capital city in the world. Hint two: This country is home to the giant weta, the world’s largest insect. Hint three: bungee jumping began here.

So where are you?”

Chile **P196**

New Zealand **P201**

South Africa **P165**

Argentina **P181**

188

You have chosen glacial meringue

"Oops," the apprentice says. "That's not right. A meringue is a sweet dessert made by whipping egg whites and sugar together. While a moraine is the pile of rocks pushed along by a glacier and then left behind when it retreats. Because you got that wrong, I've got to spin the dial and see where we end up."

"Great," Matilda says, scratching under her robe. "Then maybe we can lose these manky furs. I think you missed a flea or two."

The mention of fleas has you scratching. "Yeah let's get the next question over with before a dinosaur comes along and eats us."

The apprentice shakes his head. "Don't be silly. The dinosaurs died out around 65 million years ago. You might get trampled by a wooly mammoth or get eaten by a saber-toothed tiger, but you won't find any dinosaurs except as fossils."

"Saber-toothed tiger? You mean like Diego in that movie *Ice Age*?" Matilda asks.

"Yep. Did you know they had teeth almost 12 inches long?" the apprentice asks.

"Crikey!" Matilda says. "That's not a tooth, that's a foot! Spin that dial and let's get the heck out of here. I'm too young to be cat food."

"Okay, hold tight." He turns the dial.

BANG—FLASH!

The shock nearly knocks you off your feet. "Whoa that was a big one!" you say, regaining your balance and looking around. "Where are we? I smell fart."

"It's not fart," the apprentice says holding his nose and speaking like he's got a cold, "it's sulphur."

"Sulphur?" you repeat.

The apprentice nods. "We're in New Zealand. You know, where they filmed *Lord of the Rings.* We're just outside a town called Rotorua."

"Jeez… You mean people have to smell fart all the time?" Matilda says. "And I though using the bathroom after my dad was bad."

"You don't notice it after a while," the apprentice says. "Or so they say."

"Yuck," you say. "I can taste it in the air. Can you please give us another question before I choke?"

"Don't you want to know about New Zealand? It has

geysers and volcanoes. You can ski on them you know."

"Ski on a geyser?" Matilda says.

"No, the volcanoes," the apprentice says. "Stop being a drongo."

"I'm not a bird," Matilda says. "We have spangled drongos back home in Australia." She tucks her hands under her armpits and starts flapping her elbows like a demented chicken. "Nope, I can't fly either. Definitely not a drongo."

The apprentice rolls his eyes then reaches for his pocket. "Okay here's an easy one. If you get this wrong I'll have to spin the dial on the time machine. We could end up anywhere. But, if you get it right, you'll be nearly home. How does that sound?"

You nod. The smell in the air is getting to you. Despite having your hand over your mouth and nose, your eyes are beginning to water. "Go for it," you say quickly, before replacing your hand.

"Okay. Here we go," the apprentice says. "What are New Zealanders known as? Are they called:"

Kiwis after a flightless bird? **P186**

Or

Wallabies after the marsupial? **P181**

Back in time

"It's dark," Matilda says. "Where are we?"

"I think we're in a cave," you reply.

Standing quietly as your eyes adjust, you listen to the sounds around you. Somewhere further into the cave you hear the steady *plonk, plonk, plonk* of water dripping.

After a minute or so, you start to see shadows. A small amount of light is seeping into the cave through a crack high in the rock above you. Wisps of smoke drift up from the remnants of a fire inside a semicircle of rocks built up against one wall.

"Someone's been down here," you say. "And they haven't been gone very long by the looks of those ashes."

"Where's the apprentice?" Matilda asks, looking around nervously. "I hope he's not too far, it's chilly down here and

I'm a bit claustrophobic."

Next to the makeshift fireplace is a pile of branches. You kneel down on the ground and blow on the embers. A couple pieces glow red.

"I'll see if I can get this fire going," you say. "It'll warm us up and give us some light while we figure out what to do."

You grab one of the smaller branches and break it into pieces. These you lay gently over the embers.

"Don't smother it, mate," Matilda says. "It needs air to burn."

You purse you lips and blow. The extra oxygen makes the embers glow red-hot and before you know it, the small pile of kindling bursts into flames. Slowly, you add more twigs and branches to the growing fire.

It isn't until you look up from your task that you spot the paintings on the wall behind you.

"Whoa!" you say taking in the scene. "Matilda, look behind you!"

Matilda turns. Her eyes widen. "That's amazing!"

Matilda isn't exaggerating. The back wall of the cave, opposite the fire, is covered in simple, yet beautiful paintings. Images of deer, horses and other grazing animals stretch from one side of the cave to the other. One animal looks a bit like a giraffe. In the centre of the wall is a painting of a fire, not unlike your own. Around it, the artist has captured men, women and children dancing.

"These paintings must be really old," Matilda says, "but the colors are so bright. I've seen cave paintings in Australia similar to this, but they're always much fainter."

Then, past the picture of the people dancing, towards the far end of the wall, you see a picture of the apprentice. He is with two other people. Your mouth drops open and your hand slowly rises to point at the image. "Matilda, look! It's—it's us! The clothes are the same and the hair color, and the…"

You can see a full circle of white around Matilda's pupils when she sees the part of the painting you're indicating.

"Bleedin' heck! How is that possible?"

"I thought I'd arrive a little earlier and record our visit," a voice from the darkness says. The apprentice steps into the light. "I see you got the fire going."

"You painted that?" you ask. "But when?"

The apprentice laughs. "You don't understand space-time very well do you? I just set the sorcerer's time machine to drop me off an hour earlier so I could paint in peace before you two arrived."

"Well it's a good likeness, I'll give you that," Matilda says. "But I bet you confuse the anthropologists if they ever find this place."

"Oh well, nothing like a few mysteries to keep people guessing. I drew a spaceman in the last cave I visited, that'll really get them going."

"So where are we?" you ask.

"And what year is it?" Matilda asks.

"This is a cave in France. It will be found in about 17,000 years."

"17,000 years!" Matilda cries. "How are we going to get home from here?"

"Don't worry. Answer this next question right, and you'll be nearly home."

You shoot the apprentice a suspicious look. "You said that last time."

"It's true," the apprentice says. "You just have to get the answer right, that's all."

You kick the ground. "Okay, but how about something easy for a change?"

"I'll see what I can do. If I give you an easy question, and you get it wrong, I'll have to send you all the way back to the beginning of the maze. You sure you want that?"

"All the way back?" you ask.

"That's not a fair suck of the sav," Matilda says.

The apprentice looks confused and turns toward you. "Translation?" he says.

"It's unfair. She doesn't like it," you say.

"Sorry, Matilda. I don't make the rules," the apprentice says.

You turn and face Matilda. "What do you think? Should we go for an easy one?"

"Give it a go, mate. We're 17,000 years from home. How much worse could it get?"

You glance at the apprentice. "You did say easy didn't you?"

"Yes but 'easy' is a relative term. For a monkey, climbing a tree is easy, but for an elephant … not so much." The apprentice gives you a smile. "So, are you a monkey or an elephant?"

You're not really sure what monkeys and elephants have to do with this decision, but you do like climbing trees. Maybe that's a clue. You scratch your head and think a moment.

"Come on ya galah. Go for it." Matilda urges.

"Okay," you say to the apprentice. "We'll go for it."

"Right … here we go. This cave painting is in France. But where is France?"

Is France in South America? **P191**

Or

Is France in Europe? **P186**

Back at the laboratory

Oops!! How did that happen?

It's as if time has reversed and you're back in the lab.

"Hey, Matilda," you say over your shoulder, "looks like I got that last question wrong. We're back at the beginning of the maze."

"Oh well," she says with a shrug. "At least it will give us a chance to look at all this equipment a bit more."

Matilda scurries down between two rows of benches. "Now where was that time machine?" She mumbles. "Ah there it is."

"Matilda! Not again. You'll get us in trouble."

Matilda ignores you and starts fiddling with the dial.

"That's a bad idea," you say. "You know what happened last—"

FLASH—BANG!

"Crikey!" Matilda says with a shake of her head. "I'll never get used to that noise."

Once again the air is full of mist and Matilda looms ghostlike through the haze.

"Welcome back to 2560 B.C," the apprentice says. "Miss me?" He reaches out his hand. "You'd better give me that box, Matilda, before you do something silly."

You glare at your Australian friend. "You mean like sending us back to Egypt…AGAIN!"

"Sorry," Matilda says, blushing slightly. "I just thought—"

"Just stop!" you say, cutting her off. "Is there anything you can do?" you ask the apprentice. "My friend here isn't the brightest bulb in the box."

"Sorry, I don't make up the rules. You'll have to go thought the maze again."

Matilda smiles. "Hey lighten up. This is fun. Any chance of getting something to eat while we're here?"

"Are you *always* hungry?" the apprentice asks.

She shakes her head. "Not always, mate. Just most of the time. In fact I was once so hungry I barbequed a goanna."

"You mean those big lizards?" you ask.

"Yup," Matilda says, giving you a cheeky grin. "Tasted a bit like chicken."

The apprentice tucks the black box under his arm and reaches into his pocket for a question. "I don't think there are goannas around here. Let's try a question, maybe we'll get lucky."

"Sounds good to me," you say. "Time travel makes me hungry too. But I'm not eating goanna."

"I'm not a fan of barbequed reptile either," the apprentice says, holding up a small scrap of paper. "Okay. Here is an

198

easy one. What is the only country that is an island AND a continent? Is it:"

Australia? **P129**

Or

China? **P143**

There are 1400 seconds in one hour

"Oh dear," the apprentice says. "Now you're in for it."

"Why?" you ask, "Just because my math isn't so good?"

"No, because you didn't think to use a calculator, or a computer or something to help you out. You just guessed didn't you?"

"Yeah well—"

"Does that mean we miss out on ice cream?" Matilda asks, giving you a nasty look. "Mate! What were you thinking?"

"Sorry, Matilda. I just—"

"—hey it's all right," the apprentice says. "You'll get another chance."

Matilda smiles. "Will we?"

The apprentice nods. "I'll just ask you another question

about time. If you get it right you can have ice cream. How does that sound?"

You wipe the sweat off your forehead. Matilda can be such a pain at times. The last thing you need is her on your back. "And if I get it wrong?" you ask.

"Well, let's just say, ice cream won't be on the menu."

"Now think hard!" Matilda says. "I'll die if I don't get some ice cream soon."

"Stop it!" you say. "How am I supposed to think with you pressuring me?"

Matilda kicks the ground. "Sorry, mate. As you were."

"Okay," the apprentice says. "Now that you two have got that out of the way. Which of the following statements is correct?"

Watches were invented in Germany. **P186**

Or

Watches were invented in Australia. **P129**

Welcome to the sorcerer's office

You find yourself in a room filled with books. It's a room unlike any you've ever seen. Your eyes are drawn upward, higher and higher.

"These shelves must be a hundred feet high," you say, craning your neck to see the top.

There is no ceiling. The room is open to the sky. You can see birds circling in the sunshine and white fluffy clouds drifting by.

"Holy moly!" Matilda says tilting her head back. "Is this place awesome, or what?"

"Ahem," a voice says, bringing your view back to floor level. "So you like my office?"

Through its last few wisps of mist, you see the sorcerer's apprentice sitting behind a large wooden desk. He is wearing brightly colored robes and a pointy hat with stars and planets on it.

"Your office?" you say. "Pretty awesome office for an apprentice!"

Matilda reaches over and pulls a book from the shelf. "*The Sorcerer's Maze Jungle Trek*," she reads. "Is this one of yours?"

The apprentice nods. "They're all mine. Your adventure will be written up some day too. But before we get sidetracked, I'd better get you home."

"*You're* sending us home?" Matilda says, putting the book back. "But don't we get to meet the sorcerer?"

The apprentice snaps his fingers and two big armchairs appear. "Please have a seat. I've got something I need to tell you."

Once you and Matilda are comfortable, the apprentice snaps his fingers again and a tray of snacks appear in front of you.

"Chocolate?" the apprentice says. "Pretzels? You must be hungry after your journey."

Matilda doesn't need to be asked twice. She grabs a big handful of pretzels. "Mmmmm, thanks," she mumbles after stuffing a couple in her mouth.

The chocolate looks good, but at the moment you're more interested in what happens next. "So you'll send us home?" you say, repeating Matilda's question. "Where's the sorcerer? You said we'd get to meet him once we got through the maze."

"I am the sorcerer."

"Puwah!" Matilda spits pretzel crumbs everywhere.

"You?" you say. "But I thought—"

"—I was just an apprentice?"

"Yeah, well…"

The sorcerer smiles. "Sorry for the confusion. Normally I *would* send an apprentice out with my guests to accompany them through the maze, but I'm so short staffed at the moment I had to come out on this trip myself. I don't suppose you'd be interested in a job?"

You study the boy's expression and try to figure out if he's joking. "Me? A sorcerer's apprentice?"

He nods. "Yes, you. Your job will be to help me make up questions for my mazes.

By now Matilda has recovered. "So you've been lying to us? That's not very nice."

"Well technically I wasn't actually lying. You see, I cast a spell on myself so I'd act just like an apprentice while we were in the maze. I didn't want to spoil your experience you see. It wasn't until I got back to my office here, that I turned back into my real self."

Matilda's face scrunches up in confusion. She looks unconvinced. "Hang on, mate! If you—"

The sorcerer leans towards Matilda, peers deeply into her eyes. "Okay, I'm sorry. I shouldn't have lied."

Matilda thinks a moment, and then smiles. "Apology accepted." She picks up another pretzel. "Great nibbles by the way."

The sorcerer turns and gives you a grin. "Chocolate?"

"Did you just put a spell on Matilda?"

"No. What makes you think that?"

You study the sorcerer's face. His gaze is steady and looks directly at you. You've heard people who are lying often can't look you in the eye.

"Okay if you're sure…"

The sorcerer smiles.

Feeling better, you reach out and take some chocolate. But as the rich creamy lump melts in your mouth, you feel your eyelids drooping. It's been a long day and you're sure it's well past your normal bedtime.

*****

The next morning, when you wake up, a faint pink mist fills your bedroom and the book you were reading rests on the bed beside you. Was it all just a dream? Or did you really work your way through the sorcerer's maze?

As you ponder this question, your phone rings. You pick it up from your bedside table and swipe the screen. "Hello?"

"Is that you?" Matilda says, on the other end of the line.

"Yeah it's me. What's up?"

"Mate! You're not going to believe the dream I had last night!"

"Oh I think I might," you say.

"Ya reckon? Okay smarty-pants, have a guess then. What was it about?"

You hesitate a moment pretending to think. "Did you visit ancient Egypt by any chance, or meet a sorcerer? Did you have to answer questions to get home again?"

"Crikey!" Matilda says. "Now how the heck did you know that?"

THE END

Why not check out the List of Choices on the next page and make sure you've not missed anything important.

List of Choices

THE SORCERER'S MAZE JUNGLE TREK

(Book Three)

210

Enter the Jungle Maze

A moment ago, you were at home reading a book. When it started vibrating, you knew something was strange.

Now you're standing in the jungle, deep in the Amazon rainforest. How did that happen?

Beside you flows a slow-moving river, murky brown from all the silt it carries downstream. Monkeys screech in the trees across the water. The air is hot and buzzing with insects. As you watch a cloud of tiny flying creatures, they gather together to form words:

WELCOME, they spell in giant letters.

You blink once, then again. This day is getting crazier by the minute.

NOPE, IT'S NOT CRAZY, spell the insects. THIS IS THE START OF THE SORCERER'S MAZE.

The insect cloud bursts apart and the creatures buzz off.

You scratch your head. What's next, flying elephants?

Twenty yards away, two kids, about your age, stand beside a small boat with a little outboard motor attached to its stern, and a blue roof to protect its occupants from the hot tropical sun.

They both smile and wave.

The girl walks towards you. "Do you want a ride upriver?" she asks. "My brother and I know the Amazon well."

"Do you work for the sorcerer?" you ask. "He designed

the maze, didn't he?"

The girl nods. "Yes. My brother and I are his apprentices. The sorcerer wants you to have company while you're here."

As the two of you move down the bank to the river's edge, the girl points to the boy. "This is Rodrigo. I'm Maria."

You drop your daypack into the boat and hold out your hand. "Hi Rodrigo, interesting looking boat."

Rodrigo shakes your hand. "It does the job. But before we can go upriver," he says, pulling a piece of paper out of his pocket. "The sorcerer wants me to ask you a question. If you get it right, we can leave."

"And if not?" you ask.

"I've got more questions," the boy says, patting his pocket. "I'm sure you'll get one right eventually." Rodrigo unfolds the paper. "Okay, here's your first question. Which of the following statements is true?"

It is time to make a choice. Which do you choose?

The Amazon River has over 3000 species of fish. **P214**

Or

The Amazon River has less that 1000 species of fish. **P217**

You need to go back to the previous page and make a choice by clicking one of the links. That is how you'll work your way through the maze.

The Amazon River has over 3000 species of fish

Piranha

"Correct," Rodrigo says. "And did you know that there are catfish that grow to over 200 pounds?"

Maria smiles, "And that's not even the biggest fish here. Arapaima can grow twice that size."

"And you want me to get in that rickety boat?" you ask.

The boy laughs. "Don't worry, we'll look after you. Now help Maria push off, we've got a lot of river to cover if we're going to make it to camp by nightfall."

As Rodrigo fiddles with the engine, you help Maria push the boat into the water, watching out for piranha as you do so. There aren't any proper seats in the tiny craft, so you sit on your pack near the middle, thinking that's where it will be the safest. Maria moves to the front of the boat to act as lookout.

The outboard motor starts on the first pull and Rodrigo

points the boat away from shore. Soon you are moving upstream about twenty yards off the bank.

Birds are everywhere. The jungle is alive with tweets and squawking.

As the boat comes around a bend in the river, you see a black and white bird about the size of a chicken sitting on a branch. The bird has a big orangey-yellow bill that reminds you of a banana split lengthwise. It has black eyes and a white patch on its throat. "Hey that's a toucan, isn't it?"

"We're lucky to see one," Maria says. "They usually stay way up in the canopy."

"What do they eat?" you ask.

"Mainly fruit, but they'll eat insects and snakes or even other bird's eggs if they need to. It depends on the season."

"The rains aren't far away," the boy says, looking at the overcast sky. "During the rainy season this place changes and the river gets so wide you can barely see across it."

The girl looks back at you. In her hand is a piece of paper. "And that leads us to our next question."

The boy slows the boat down. "Sorry, but if you get it wrong, I'll have to put you ashore."

You shoot a look towards the boy. "What? Here in the middle of the jungle?"

He nods, pointing to a track leading into the dense foliage on the near bank. "Don't worry. There's a track that leads to our next stop. You'll be able to rejoin us there."

You shrug. "Okay. What's the question?"

Maria reads the question carefully. "Approximately how

216

many inches of rain fall in the Amazon Basin each year?"

You scratch your head. How much rain does fall each year? It must be quite a bit if the river gets really wide.

It is time to make a choice.

Do 100 inches of rain fall each year? **P219**

Or:

Do 400 inches of rain fall each year? **P220**

The Amazon River has less than 1000 species of fish

"Unfortunately that's not right," Maria says. "The Amazon River has over 3000 known species of fish, and scientists are finding more each year."

"I never would have guessed that many," you say.

"I know. Not many people do. Don't worry, I have plenty more questions. I'm sure you'll get the next one right."

Another boat passes by, heading downstream. It's loaded with fruit for the market in a village downstream. The people in the boat wave as they pass.

Seeing all that food has made you hungry. You reach into the side pocket of your pack, pulling out a bar of chocolate. "Would you like some?"

Maria's teeth flash white against her caramel-colored skin. "Did you know that chocolate comes from the bean of the cacao tree which originated here in South America?"

"Really?" you say, unwrapping the bar.

Maria nods. "Now it's grown in tropical countries all over the world, but it started right here." Maria sweeps her arm indicating the jungle.

The boy and girl each take a piece of chocolate and bite into it. Their eyes sparkle.

The chocolate is soft and gooey from the tropical heat. It melts in your mouth.

"Seeing you've given us some chocolate," Maria says. "We'll give you another chance to answer that last question. Just don't tell the sorcerer."

218

"My lips are sealed." You smile and stuff the empty wrapper into your pocket.

Maria smiles and reads the question again. "So which is right?"

The Amazon River has less than 1000 species of fish. **P217**

Or

The Amazon River has over 3000 species of fish. **P214**

You have chosen 100 inches of rain

"That's a shame," Maria says. "We get over 400 inches of rain. Now we have to make you walk for a while."

"But…"

She looks a bit sad. "It's not up to us. The sorcerer makes the rules."

Rodrigo turns the boat towards shore. "Don't worry. If you follow the track, you'll get to where we're having lunch. Then you can ride with us again."

You step off the boat and scramble up the bank. By the time you turn around, the boat is already moving upstream.

The track is narrow and crowded with trees and shrubs. After walking for thirty yards or so, the jungle is so dense that you can no longer see the river, or hear the sound of the outboard.

When you come to a junction, you wonder which way to go.

It is time to make a decision. Do you go:

Left towards the sound of parrots screeching? **P222**

Or

Right towards where the jungle seems more open. **P233**

You have chosen 400 inches of rain

"Wow, you're good," Rodrigo says. "The Amazon's rainy season is from December to May. Boy, does it rain! Over 400 inches a year!"

You do some quick calculations in your head, dividing 400 by 12. "That's over 33 feet!" you say.

Maria nods in agreement. "Did you know that about twenty percent of all the fresh water that goes into the world's oceans comes from this one river?

"It's hard to imagine that amount of rain," you say. "Maybe we should set up an umbrella shop."

Maria smiles.

"The Amazon basin drains the land from over 7 million square miles," Rodrigo says. "No wonder it pumps out so much water."

"Look!" Rodrigo points to a snake lying in the shallow water near the bank. "I bet you can't guess the name of that animal."

The snake is a golden color with black stripes on its head.

"Wow that's big," you say.

Rodrigo grins. "About as big as they get," he says, swerving the boat for you to have a closer look. "If you get this next question right, you get to move on through the maze."

"And let me guess," you say. "If I get it wrong, you feed me to the snake?"

"Ha!" Maria laughs, "No, we'll just make you walk."

"So, what sort of snake is it?" Rodrigo asks.

It is time to make a decision. What do you think?

Is it:

A rattlesnake? **P224**

Or

An anaconda? **P231**

222

You have chosen left towards the sound of parrots

After turning left, you push through a few overhanging fronds towards the sound of parrots. As the squawking gets louder, you remember reading that some of the parrots living in the Amazonia rainforest are good mimics, which is why people like them as pets.

When you see a group of green birds sitting on a tree in a small clearing, you pull out your camera and take a few shots.

"Hello birdies," you call out to them, wondering if they'll reply.

One of the birds turns its head sideways and stares at your. Then it bounces up and down on its perch. "Hello birdie!" it squawks. "Hello birdie!"

You walk around the tree watching the birds, and then decide you'd better get going if you're ever going to catch up with the boat. Your stomach rumbles, reminding you that lunch isn't far away.

But which way do you go? There are four tracks leading out of the clearing.

You try to remember the turns you've taken and decide, as an aid to navigation, to pretend that the clearing is a clock face. You call the path you entered the clearing on the 6 o'clock path. There are other paths leading out of the clearing at 9 o'clock, 12 o'clock and 3 o'clock. But which do you take?

You are thinking hard, when you hear something large crashing through the jungle behind you. It could be a jaguar. There is no time to waste! Quick, which path do you choose?

Take the 9 o'clock path. **P236**

Take the 12 o'clock path. **P238**

Take the 3 o'clock path. **P240**

224

You have chosen Rattlesnake

"Oops," Rodrigo says. "There is a type of rattlesnake that lives in South America, but that beast over there is an anaconda."

"Let me guess," you say. "It's the biggest snake in the world."

Maria giggles. "How did you know?"

"Everything's big around here. Giant fish, giant otters, giant snakes. I suppose you'll show me the world's biggest spider next."

Maria raises her eyebrows. "That can be arranged."

"I was joking!" you say.

"Too late," Rodrigo says. "Look behind you."

Your eyes move first. Then you slowly turn your head and look around. "I hope you're kidding."

"The sorcerer aims to please," Rodrigo says looking down.

You follow his eyes and spot a hairy leg sticking out from under your pack in the bottom of the boat. Then you see another and another as the spider crawls out.

"Holy moly! What is it?" you say looking at the hairy black body. "It must be a foot long!"

Rodrigo nods. "It's a Goliath birdeater."

"Birdeater?" you say, moving further away from the hairy beast.

"It can also eat small rodents, lizards and frogs," Rodrigo says. "It has fangs an inch long."

As if the size of the spider wasn't enough to scare you, the thing starts hissing at you.

"Oh that's creepy! Can't you make it go away?" you say.

"Don't worry they're not deadly to people," Maria says pulling a piece of paper from her pocket. "Unless you're allergic." She raises her eyebrows. "Are you allergic?"

"How should I know?" you say, standing on your tip toes. "Just get rid of it!"

"Sure. All you have to do is answer this question."

"Okay," you say. "But read it quickly."

"Okay. Here it is. How does the Goliath birdeater make its hissing sound? Is it by:"

Releasing air out of its mouth? **P226**

Or

Rubbing its legs together? **P228**

You think the tarantula releases air to hiss

"Unfortunately that answer is incorrect," Maria says. "The tarantula makes a hissing sound by rubbing its legs together. But you're not the first to get that one wrong."

The spider runs towards you with a speed that rocks you back on your heels.

You are about to jump into the water when Rodrigo pushes it away with his oar.

"Phew!" you say. "That was scary."

"Imagine how you'd feel if you were a little mouse," Maria says.

After a moment, you stop shaking. "So what now? Are you going to put me ashore?"

Maria laughs. "Not this time. That was a pretty tough question."

You breathe a sigh of relief.

"But I am going to ask you another question. If you get this one wrong, you'll have to go back to the very beginning of the maze."

"Okay," you say. "Just promise to keep that spider away."

"I can't promise anything. It's the sorcerer that makes the rules," Maria says. "But I don't know why you're so worried. The poor spider's probably more afraid of you than you are of it."

You hand is still shaking. "I'm not so sure about that."

Rodrigo laughs nervously. "I'm not that fond of spiders either, so think carefully."

Maria pulls another question out of her pocket. “Okay here’s an easy one. How many legs does a spider have? Is it:”

8 legs? **P228**

Or

6 legs? **P230**

Tarantulas hiss by rubbing two of its 8 legs together

"That's right. Tarantulas hiss by rubbing two of its 8 legs together," Maria says. "Did you know that you can always tell a spider from an insect by counting its legs? Spiders are arachnids with eight legs. Insects only have six."

"What are millipedes?" you ask. "Are they insects? They have heaps of legs."

Maria looks confused. "Hmm... I might have to ask the sorcerer about that one."

"I might do a search online about it when I get home," you say. "Insects sound interesting."

The tarantula crawls up the side of the boat. Rodrigo picks it up with the end of his oar and flicks it onto the shore. "They're all just bugs to me," he says. "They belong in the jungle, not on my boat."

You nod in agreement. "You're telling me."

Rodrigo, no longer distracted by the big spider, accelerates the boat and cruises along a row of trees overhanging the bank. "There are some good spots to see parrots around here," he says.

Now that sounds more like it. Parrots are your favorite birds. You've always wanted to own a parrot, so you could teach it to talk.

Half an hour later, Rodrigo nudges the boat into bank. "Here's where you get off if you want to see parrots."

You step ashore and scramble up.

"Just follow the track," he says. "It will lead you to where we're going to have lunch. We'll meet you there."

You wave goodbye and head into the jungle in search of birds, your camera at the ready.

The track is narrow and crowded with trees and shrubs. After walking for thirty yards or so, the jungle is so dense that you can no longer see the river, or hear the sound of the outboard.

When you come to a junction you wonder which way to go.

It is time to make a decision. Do you go:

Left towards the sound of parrots screeching? **P222**

Or

Right towards where the jungle seems more open. **P233**

230

Oops! You're back at the beginning at the maze!

How did that happen? You must have answered that last question wrong.

You are back at the clearing beside the river. Rodrigo smiles and waves as if he's never seen you before.

Maria walks towards you. "Want a ride up river?" she says. "My brother and I are trained guides."

"You work for the sorcerer." you say.

She looks confused. "How did you know?"

You shake your head in confusion as the two of you walk back down to the river's edge. You've been here before, but they don't seem to know you. You drop your daypack into the boat.

"Before we go upriver," Rodrigo says, pulling a piece of paper out of his pocket. "The sorcerer wants me to ask you a question. If you get it right, we can leave."

"And if not?" you ask, hoping you'll get the same question as last time.

"We'll just have to wait and see, won't we?" he says with a grin. "Okay, which of these statements is true?"

The Amazon River has over 3000 species of fish. **P214**

Or

The Amazon River has less than 1000 species of fish. **P217**

You have chosen Anaconda.

"Well done," Rodrigo says. "Anaconda is correct."

"Phew!" you say. "That's good, I didn't want to walk. There's so much more to see from the river."

"That's true," Rodrigo says. "But you still have a few more things to do before I can take you further upriver."

You're not too worried about more questions. You've been doing pretty well so far so you have no reason to think you won't continue to get the right answers.

"For your next challenge, I've got to put you ashore," says Rodrigo. "But don't worry; you can meet up with us again further upriver."

He nudges the boat into the riverbank and you scramble up.

"Where do I go?" you call to them.

"Just follow the path up the river," Maria says. "And try not to get lost. We'll see you at camp."

You don't like the sound of this much. "But what if I *do* get lost?"

The two of them laugh.

Maria shoves the boat away from the bank with an oar as Rodrigo starts the motor again. "Don't worry," she says. "The sorcerer will send a parrot to find you if it starts to get dark before you arrive."

The sorcerer will send a parrot? Why doesn't that comfort you? You lean forward and peer into the jungle. The path looks like a tunnel, with little light filtering down through the thick canopy.

When you turn back, the blue boat is disappearing around the corner, heading upriver.

"Oh well," you say to yourself. "I'd better get moving."

You follow the path until you come to a small clearing. In its center is a tree with a line of green birds sitting along one of its branch.

"Hello birdies," you call out to them, wondering if they'll reply.

"Hello birdie," one of them repeats, bouncing up and down on its perch.

After chatting with the birds for a few minutes, you decide you'd better get going if you're ever going to catch up with the boat. Your stomach is rumbling. You hope they've got some food onboard.

But which way do you go? The clearing is like a clock face with tracks at 12 o'clock, 3 o'clock, 9 o'clock and the one you came in on at 6 o'clock. Which trail will lead you along the river towards camp?

It is time to make a decision. Which one of these three paths do you take?

Take the 9 o'clock path. **P236**

Take the 12 o'clock path. **P238**

Take the 3 o'clock path. **P240**

You have chosen right towards open jungle.

The path here is sunnier and more open. Parrots screech all around you as flashes of red, green, blue and yellow flit through the canopy.

After walking for about twenty minutes, you come to a big tree with a large branch hanging over the path. On it sits three birds.

At one end is a bird with teal-blue wings, a green patch on his head, and a yellow body.

"Macaw!" the bird squawks.

"Yes you are," you say. "A Blue and Gold Macaw."

The next bird along the branch is a brilliantly-blue bird with circles of yellow around its eyes and a flash of yellow on its face by its black curved beak.

"Macaw!" the bird screams.

"Yes you are!" you say to the beautiful bird. "You're a Hyacinth Macaw."

The birds bob up and down, looking at you. Then both birds turn to the third bird. This one has a red head and shoulders, and green, yellow and blue back and wings. You've seen pictures of this bird before, but have never seen so many colors on one bird in real life.

The bird looks down at you and squawks, "Macaw!"

"Yes you are," you say. "You're a beautiful Scarlet Macaw."

You whip out your camera. Nobody at home is going to believe you've taken a picture of three beautiful parrots all on the same branch!

"Macaw!" the first bird says.

"Macaw," the second bird says.

"Better get a move on!" the Scarlet Macaw says.

Did you hear right? Is that Macaw telling you to hurry up, or is the sorcerer playing mind games with you? In any case, the bird is right. You'd better get a move on if you're going to catch up with Maria and Rodrigo.

You head back into the jungle in a direction you think will lead you upstream. Ten minutes later, you come into another clearing where a group of green birds with yellow crowns sit on a bush. You point your camera and take a few shots.

These are Yellow-Crested Amazons.

"Hello birdies," you call out to them, wondering if they'll reply.

After photographing the birds for a few minutes, you decide you'd better get going.

But which way do you go? There are four tracks leading in and out of the clearing.

As an aid to navigation, you pretend that the clearing is a clock face.

You call the path you came in on the 6 o'clock path. There are other paths leading out of the clearing at 9 o'clock, 12 o'clock and 3 o'clock.

But which do you take?

As you wonder which way to go, you hear a large animal crashing through the jungle behind you.

Is it following your scent?
There is no time to waste!
Quick, which path do you choose?
Take the 9 o'clock path. **P236**
Take the 12 o'clock path. **P238**
Take the 3 o'clock path. **P240**

You have chosen the 9 o'clock path.

After a sip of water, you head out of the clearing, determined to catch up with the boat. You pick up your pace, sure that the path you've chosen will lead you back to the river. The path turns left, then winds around to the right.

Before long, the path narrows and you're not so certain you're going the right way after all.

After walking around another twenty yards, you pull aside a fern frond and hear a familiar voice.

"Hello birdie," a parrot says as you come into the clearing.

It's the same clearing you left only half an hour ago. How did that happen? You must have walked in a circle.

But which way do you go now? Which path is which? Is the 6 o'clock path still the 6 o'clock path or is it now the 12 o'clock path?

You head is spinning and you're wasting time turning around and around in circles.

"Better get a move on!" one of the parrots says.

You look up at a big fat green parrot sitting on a nearby branch. "What did you say?"

"Hello birdie," the bird says.

Maybe you're just hearing things.

"6 o'clock. Time for the news," another parrot says.

Is the sorcerer playing mind games with you? Or is the bird smarter than it looks?

None the less, the bird is right. You'd better get a move on.

But which way do you go? And which path do you take?

Do you:

Take the 12 o'clock path? **P238**

Take the 3 o'clock path? **P240**

Take the 6 o'clock path? **P242**

You have chosen the 12 o'clock path.

The sound of birds and bugs surround you. Small animal rustle through the undergrowth. You keep a sharp watch for potential danger as you move swiftly along the path. Suddenly, there is a crashing sound off to your right. Is something stalking you? And more to the point, is it dangerous?

Thinking of all the dangerous animals that live in the Amazonian rainforest just makes you more scared. Then you remember that mosquitoes, and the diseases they carry, harm more people than all the other animals put together each year. At least you can do something about that.

You stop, pull a tube out of your daypack and cover the bare patches of your skin with insect repellent before heading off again.

Every few moments you stop and listen for the sound of water, but the path winds around so much it's hard to know which direction you're going. Then after half an hour or so, you hear parrots.

A few minutes later your worst fears are confirmed: You are back at the clearing.

"Hello birdie," a parrot says in greeting. "Better get a move on."

But which way do you try next?

You look right, then left, then turn all the way around trying to figure out which path will lead you to the river.

You hold your hand up to your ear and listen, but all you

can here are the sounds of the jungle, the hum of insects and something snapping branches behind you.

It is time to make a decision. Which path do you take?

Take the 9 o'clock path. **P236**

Take the 3 o'clock path. **P240**

Take the 6 o'clock path. **P242**

You have chosen the 3 o'clock path.

Leaving the parrots behind, you head off into the jungle. It isn't long before the path narrows and starts to climb. If the path is climbing, you must be heading further away from the river. Not at all what you wanted.

The ground underfoot is damp and covered in leaf litter from all the trees.

You are starting to worry when at last the ground starts to head back down again. Maybe you've chosen the right path after all.

When you turn a last corner, you hear a voice.

"Hello birdie," it says.

Pulling a branch aside you find you've gone around in a big circle and are back at the clearing again.

"Hello birdie," another parrot says.

It's funny hearing the parrot talking, but you're concerned about the time you've wasted.

Which path should you take this time? You're well and truly stuck in the sorcerer's maze.

You went out on the 3 o'clock path, so you must have come back in on one of the others. But which is which? All you've managed to do is turn yourself around and lose all sense of direction. You are standing in the middle of the clearing, turning around and around wondering which way to go.

"Hello birdie," one of the parrots says. "Better get a move on."

The bird is right. You had better get a move on if you're going to catch up with Maria and Rodrigo.

Which of the paths do you take this time?

Take the 9 o'clock path. **P236**

Take the 12 o'clock path. **P238**

Take the 6 o'clock path. **P242**

You have chosen the 6 o'clock path.

This path looks like all the others. In fact, you're pretty sure you've been here before. But then you hear faint splashes ahead of you. Is it the river?

Excited to have found the river at last you start jogging. The splashing in the river gets louder and louder. But what's making the noise? Is it an animal or people?

You pull some low hanging branches aside and peer out over the river. There is something large and pink, in the water off to your left. You wait till it surfaces again. Then you see what it is. It's one of the rare pink river dolphins. So beautiful… You stand transfixed as the creature darts back and forth catching its lunch.

When you scramble along the path for a clearer view, you discover Maria and Rodrigo sitting on a log preparing food.

"So you made it," Maria says. "We always stop here to watch the dolphins."

"Not many of them left unfortunately," Rodrigo says. "Would you like something to eat?"

It feels like you've been walking for hours. You take the piece of yellow-green fruit the boy offers and bite right in. It's about the size of a tennis ball. The flesh is pink and sweet. Juice runs down your chin.

"Mmmm… that's good," you say. "What do you call it?"

"Ah now there's a question if ever I heard one," Rodrigo says, his eyes twinkling.

You hear the girl laugh as she pulls a piece of paper out of her pocket. “Yes, I seem to have a question on that topic right here.”

“I should have known.” You groan and take another bite. “But if you give me another one of these, I’ll answer all the questions you like.”

Rodrigo tosses you another piece of fruit.

“Okay,” Maria says. “If you want a ride in the boat, all you have to do is name the fruit you’re eating.”

It is time to make a choice. Did you just eat a:

Plantain? **P244**

Or a:

Guava? **P246**

You have chosen plantain.

Well as you can see, plantains are like bananas and not the shape of a tennis ball at all. The correct answer was guava. Plantains are a very important fruit for those living in the Amazon basin. Often they are roasted on an open fire or cut lengthwise and fried.

"Looks like you're still walking," Maria says. "That's a shame. I was enjoying your company."

"Couldn't I have another question?" you ask.

The two of them whisper in each other's ear for a moment.

It's Rodrigo that speaks first. "Okay we can give you another question, but if you get it wrong you'll have to go all the way to the beginning of the maze.

"All the way?"

He nods. "Still interested?"

You think a moment. "Yes," you say. "Surely I can't get

two in a row wrong."

"Okay, here it is. What is the name of the largest predator in the Amazon basin?"

Is it the:

Black caiman? **P250**

Or

Tiger shark? **P256**

You have chosen guava.

"Looks like you get to ride in the boat again," Maria says. "Guava is correct."

"Birds like them too," her brother says. "And the monkeys."

You smile. "Well I'm not surprised, they're delicious."

After the three of you finish eating, Rodrigo and Maria return to the boat.

You rinse your hands in the river and climb aboard. "So, will we see many monkeys as we head up river?"

Maria nods. "You like monkeys?"

"And birds," you reply. "I saw some parrots in the jungle when I was walking."

Just as Rodrigo is about to say something, a brown furry face pokes out of the water about 20 yards away.

He points. "Hey look, it's an otter."

"Wow, that's huge!" you say.

Maria laughs. "They don't call them giant otters for nothing. They're the biggest in the whole world."

You're not surprised. This one looks about six feet long and weighs more than you do. "I thought they were endangered?"

"They are," Rodrigo says. "But the sorcerer asked this one to visit us so you could see how amazing they are."

The face dives under the water. Thirty seconds later, the otter back holding a fish between its paws. Floating on its back, it bites into its lunch.

"As you can see, they eat a lot of fish," Maria says. "A big one can eat 10 pounds in a single day!"

After the otter finishes the fish, it swims closer to the boat.

"They're inquisitive animals," Rodrigo says. "Unfortunately hunters nearly wiped them out for their fur."

"Destroying their habitat doesn't help either," the girl says. "People need to think more about the animals before they chop down the forest or build mines."

As you watch the otter, it is joined by four more. "Hey look. The rest of the family has arrived."

Rodrigo points to a hole in the river bank. "I think that's one of their dens over there. They live in big family groups."

Maria laughs as the otters frolic in the water.

"Anyway, it's time to go," Rodrigo says. "We've still got some distance to make before we get to camp.

When the motor starts, the otters swim off in search of more fish and Rodrigo points the bow of the boat back out into the river.

You sit down on your pack and watch the miles flow past.

"So you'd like to see some monkeys?"Maria says as she sits down beside you. "Any particular favorites?"

"Spider monkeys are cute," you reply. "I like chimpanzees too, but they're only in Africa."

"We also have lots of marmosets, dozens of different tamarins, howler monkeys and squirrel monkeys," she says. "Squirrel monkeys live in big groups."

"That's right," Rodrigo says. "I saw a group of about 500 squirrel monkeys once."

"That's the population of a small town," you say.

"Squirrel monkeys are small though," Maria says. "You could hold a full grown one in the palm of your hand."

You hold out your palm and try to imagine a monkey sitting there. "Wow that is small. I have so many questions. Maybe you could answer some of them?"

"Speaking of which," Rodrigo says. "If you want to get through this maze, it's time to answer another one."

You sigh. "Or you'll put me ashore?"

"Sorry," he says with a shrug.

"Okay, let's get it over with. What's the question?"

He pulls a piece of paper out of his pocket. "This one is more of a riddle, so listen carefully."

You nod.

"Right. If you start with 3 spider monkeys, add 4 tamarins and 3 squirrel monkeys, what is the total number of appendages the monkeys have?"

"Hmmm, appendages. Aren't they arms and legs?

"Maybe," he says. "It's certainly something that can grab hold of things."

"Okay," you say. "Let me think a moment."

It is time to make a decision.

Do 3 spider monkeys, 4 tamarins, and 3 squirrel monkeys have:

40 appendages in total? **P257**

Or

50 appendages? **P254**

You have chosen black caiman.

"Correct! Looks like you get to ride in the boat again," Maria says.

You pump the air with your fist. "Yes!"

Maria giggles. "Did you know that black caiman can grow up to sixteen feet long? Their black scaly skin acts as camouflage when they're hunting prey along the river."

"Sixteen feet long? Wow, that's big," you say.

"Females can lay up to 65 eggs at a time. Now's about the right time of year too, just before the rainy season. The eggs take about six weeks to hatch."

Once the three of you have finished eating your lunch, the Rodrigo and Maria return to the boat.

You rinse you hands in the river, then help Maria push the boat into the water and climb aboard. "Will we see many monkeys as we head up river?"

Maria nods. "Heaps!"

"Excellent. I love monkeys … and birds," you say. "There were lots of parrots in the jungle."

Just as Rodrigo is about to say something, a brown furry face pokes out of the water about 20 yards away. "Hey look, it's an otter."

"Oh that's so cute! And big!" you say.

Maria laughs. "They don't call them giant otters for nothing! They're the largest otter in the whole world."

You're not surprised. This one looks bigger than you. "I thought they were endangered?"

"They are," Rodrigo says. "But the sorcerer wanted you to have a treat."

The otter dives under the water. Thirty seconds later, it's back holding a fish between its paws. Then it throws the fish into your boat and dives again.

"Looks like dinner is sorted," Rodrigo says.

"The otter resurfaces, floats on its back and bites into its lunch.

"As you can see, they eat a lot of fish," Maria says. "A big otter can eat 10 pounds in a single day."

After the otter finishes eating, it swims closer to the boat.

"They're inquisitive animals," the Rodrigo says. "Unfortunately hunters nearly wiped them out for their fur."

"Destroying their habitat doesn't help," his sister says. "People need to think more about the animals before they chop down the forest or start mining."

The otter flips over and dives again.

"Anyway, it's time to go," Rodrigo says, we've still got a

few miles to travel before we get to camp. He pulls the cord and starts the motor.

As the otter surfaces with another fish, Rodrigo points the bow of the boat back out into the river.

"So you'd like to see some monkeys?" Maria says. "Any particular favorites?"

"Spider monkeys are cute," you reply, "and golden tamarins."

"We also have lots of marmosets, dozens of different tamarins, howler monkeys and squirrel monkeys," she says. "Squirrel monkeys live in big groups."

"That's right," her brother says. "I saw one troupe of squirrel monkeys that must have had 500 in it."

"That's not a troupe," you say. "That's a crowd."

"Squirrel monkeys are small though," the girl says. "You could hold a full grown monkey in the palm of your hand."

"Really? I have so many questions I'd like to ask you about them," you say.

"Speaking of which," Rodrigo says. "If you want to get through this maze, it's time to answer another one."

"Or you'll put me ashore again, I suppose?"

"Sorry," he says. "But it's the sorcerer who makes the rules, not me."

"Okay, so what's the question?"

He pulls a piece of paper out of his pocket. "This one is more of a riddle, so listen carefully."

You nod.

Rodrigo reads. "If you start with 3 spider monkeys and

add 4 tamarins and 3 squirrel monkeys, what is the total number of appendages the monkeys have?"

Do they have:

40 appendages in total? **P257**

Or

50 appendages? **P254**

254

You have chosen that the monkeys have 50 appendages.

"Well done," Maria says. "Most of the people who've come into the maze forget that a monkey's tail is an appendage too. They're not just arms and legs you know."

As Rodrigo steers the boat further upstream Maria shows you a picture of a golden lion tamarin. "Some people think tamarins are a type of fruit and not a monkey."

"Sounds a bit like mandarins." you say, "so I'm not surprised"

"It does." Maria says. "And tamarind, the fruit has a 'd' at the end."

You stare at the monkeys. "They look about the size of a squirrel."

"I suppose they are," Maria says. "But there are quite a few different types. I like the emperor tamarin best, with its funny white mustache."

"Tamarins are pretty," Rodrigo says as he scans the river bank, looking for more animals. "But if you're looking for color, the birds win hands down."

The area around the river is a busy place. Birds chirp and squawk nearby and you hear splashes further upstream. You're pleased to be in the boat when Rodrigo points out a shoal of piranha attacking something in the water up ahead.

"Looks like a dead capybara," he says. "Piranha are a lot less vicious than the movies make out. They rarely attack larger animals unless they are already dead or dying."

"Really? What about people?" you ask. "I thought they

could strip you to the bone in minutes."

The girl smiles and shakes her head. "Hollywood has a lot to answer for. Piranhas swim in groups, mainly for their own protection. There's safety in numbers when you're a fish. But even so, they're often eaten by caimans, birds and otters."

"What's a caiman?" you ask.

The boy smiles and reaches into his pocket. "It just so happens I've got a question that relates to that."

You should have known. Every time you ask a question, these two sorcerer's apprentices come back with one of their own.

As you watch the piranha finish off the capybara, the boy gives you a serious look. "If you get this next question you can go to our jungle camp."

"What happens if I get it wrong?" you ask.

The boys points to shore. "Back into the jungle on foot I'm afraid."

You cross your fingers behind your back and hope the question isn't too hard. Some time in camp and a bit of a rest, sound just what you need.

"Okay, here we go. Caiman are the largest predator in the Amazon basin. But are caiman related to alligators or sharks?"

It is time to make a decision. What do you say?

Caiman are related to sharks. **P256**

Or

Caiman are related to alligators. **P258**

Oops. That's wrong. You are back in the jungle.

In a puff of smoke, you find yourself back in the clearing with the parrots.

"Hello birdie," a parrot says

"Hello birdie," you reply. "Now get lost."

"Get lost. Get lost. Get lost!" the parrot repeats, bouncing up and down on his branch.

"Quiet birdie, I'm trying to think."

"Quiet birdie!" the parrot squawks. "Quiet birdie. Quiet birdie. Better get moving!"

The bird is right. You'd better get moving.

But which way do you go? Which path is which? You're all turned around again.

Do you:

take the 12 o'clock path? **P238**

take the 3 o'clock path? **P240**

take the 6 o'clock path? **P242**

take the 9 o'clock path? **P236**

Oops. 40 appendages is wrong.

Rodrigo pull a picture of a spider monkey out of his pocker. "What about the tails?" he says pointing at the monkey's backside. "Tails are appendages too. Now I've got to send you back."

"Do you really?" You ask.

He nods. "At least you'll find a friend there."

"Will I?"

He smiles. "Yep."

In a puff of smoke, you are back in the jungle clearing with the parrots.

"Hello birdie!"

The boy was right. Your old friend the parrot is here.

"Hello, hello, hello," the parrot says as it bounces up and down on its branch. "You'd better get moving."

But which way do you go? Which path is which? You're all turned around and every path looks the same.

Do you:

take the 12 o'clock path? **P238**

take the 3 o'clock path? **P240**

take the 6 o'clock path? **P242**

take the 9 o'clock path? **P236**

Welcome to Camp 1

"Welcome to Camp 1," Rodrigo and Maria say in unison.

You smile as you look around. The place is pretty basic. Green tarpaulins are strung up between the trees with nylon cord to provide shade.

A wooden crate filled with cans of food and cooking utensils sits on the ground next to a campfire. A picnic table with bench seats sits nearby and acts as camp kitchen and dining room. Pitched off to one side of the covered area is a large tent with mosquito netting on its windows.

Maria smiles and walks towards an ice chest sitting under the table. "Like a cold soda?"

With a rattle of ice cubes she pulls out a bottle. Beads of moisture run down the bottle's side.

"How did you get ice way out here in the middle of the Amazonia rainforest?" you ask.

Rodrigo laughs. "It's the sorcerer, silly. He just snaps his fingers and things appear."

"Saves going to the supermarket I suppose." You take a soda and raising it to your lips. "Ahhhh, that is so good."

Maria and Rodrigo grab a soda each and the three of you sit down at the picnic table.

"So what now?" you ask.

You glance down as Rodrigo pulls yet another piece of paper out of his pocket. "Have you got an endless supply of questions in there?"

"I'm not sure," he says. "They just appear whenever I need one. The sorcerer's pretty good at this maze stuff."

You have to admit that the questions you've had so far have been interesting. "So what is it this time? More about animals?"

Rodrigo shakes his head. "No this one is about… Well you'll see. I'd hate to ruin the surprise. If you get it right you get to sleep in the tent."

"And if I get it wrong?"

He shrugs. "I'm not quite sure. We'll just have to wait and find out."

"Are you sure you don't know?" you ask, searching Rodrigo's face.

"I promise," he says. "I'm just an apprentice. The sorcerer only tells me what I need to know. Sometimes I'm as surprised as you are with what happens."

Spreading out the piece of paper on the table in front of him, Rodrigo starts reading. "Okay here we go. Brazil is the world's largest producer of what common product? Is it:"

Coffee? **P260**

Or is it

Tea? **P278**

You have chosen coffee.

"Well done!" Rodrigo says. "On the other side of the question paper is a picture of a coffee plant. Brazil has over 10,000 square miles of coffee plantations. That's quite a lot don't you think?"

"Yeah I suppose it is," you say. "Doesn't China produce the most tea?"

Rodrigo nods. "Yep." He walks over to the tent and lifts the flap. "Now you can make yourself comfortable, away from the mosquitoes. We'll be leaving camp early so I hope you sleep well."

"What about you and Maria?" you ask Rodrigo. "Where will you stay?"

"When the sorcerer snaps his fingers, we'll be transported home for the night," he says.

"You mean I'll be here alone?"

"I'm afraid so," Rodrigo says. "But don't worry. At least you won't be sleeping in the open. I've even left you some sandwiches in case you get hungry."

Things could be worse. You step inside the tent and look around. There is a camp bed with a thin mattress and a flashlight. Nothing else.

"What about blankets or a sleeping bag?" you ask.

"Way too warm for that," Rodrigo says with a chuckle. "We're almost at the equator. It's nearly as hot at night as it is during the day."

You try out the bed. "Not bad — for the middle of

nowhere."

After eating a sandwich, you lay on the bed and close your eyes, planning on having a five minute nap before going back outside to where Rodrigo and Maria are sitting at the table cooking pieces of fish on long sticks over the fire. But when you open your eyes again, it is dark and you can hear rustling in the jungle all around you.

"Rodrigo?" you call out. "Maria?"

There is no reply.

You figure the sorcerer must have snapped his fingers and whisked them home.

Quietly, you sit and listen to the sounds of the jungle.

The frogs are the loudest. If you listen carefully, you can hear at least ten different calls.

Some sound almost like crickets chirping, while others are deep booming rumbles.

On the ground, sitting on your empty soda bottle is a little green frog. It stares up at you with big black eyes.

"Ribbet!" the frog says.

After a few more croaks, the frog springs towards you. But rather than landing on you, there is a puff of smoke and the frog turns into a piece of paper which flutters down onto your lap.

You look at the paper expecting another question from the sorcerer, but there are only letters on the page.

And not just one or two letters, but a whole block of them!

It doesn't seem to make any sense.

262

Or does it?

ueieuyjmdnikloksłksj
oieioejlookaroundjkd
slookoopoeedds;woej
dkdfjedklookarounds
slslookaroundklitvxjf
aledkdxmksieurtedlljk

After staring at the paper for a few minutes, you hear something rustling around the camp. You're unsure of what to do. It is time to make a decision. Should you:

Look around? **P263**

Or

Go back to sleep? **P276**

You have chosen to look around.

You've seen the secret message in the block of letters so you grab the flashlight and start looking around. It is pitch black apart from the dull glow of the fire. You throw on a few more logs and sit at the table.

Suddenly the frogs go quiet. Has something disturbed them? You sit a still as a rock and listen. There is rustling in the jungle not more than ten yards away.

Your eyes strain as you peer into the darkness. The shadows make all sorts of shapes. Did something just move? Lying beside the fire is a branch used for poking the embers. You stretch down and grab it.

Holding its blackened point towards the source of the noise, you hold your breath, expecting a wild beast to come charging forward at any moment. Then, after another rustle, you see a pair of golden eyes peering back at you.

Is it a jaguar? Are you about to become animal food?

Holding the stick like a spear, you huddle closer to the fire, never taking your eyes off the pair of eyes staring back at you.

"Meow!"

What? That doesn't sound like a jaguar.

Then you see it. It's a black housecat. How did a cat get out here in the jungle? You crouch down and hold out your hand. "Here puss, puss, puss."

The cat runs over and rubs its face against your hand. Then it starts purring.

"What are you doing out here kitty?" you ask.

The cat sits and looks up at you. It's as if it understands what you are saying.

"Are you the sorcerer's cat?" you ask.

"Meow," says the cat, rubbing against you once more.

"Did the sorcerer send you here to give me a message?"

The cat springs forward and, in a puff of gray smoke turns into a paper airplane which flies around in a big loop and then plonks into your lap. You unfold the paper. You suspect it's going to be another question about Brazil. But you're wrong. There are numbers on the page. It's a math problem with four numbers and a blank space. The note says:

WHAT IS THE NEXT NUMBER IN THIS SEQUENCE?
ANSWER CORRECTLY AND YOU'RE IN FOR A BIG SURPRISE.
GET IT WRONG AND YOU HAVE TO GO BACK
TO THE BEGINNING OF THIS LEVEL.

2 …4 …8 … 16 …__?

Is it:

22 **P295**

24 **P303**

32 **P284**

36 **P295**

What animal is this?

Maria giggles. “Oops. Looks like you’re back at the start. I thought you said you knew animals?”

“I do normally,” you say scratching your head.

“At least you get another go. So, do you remember what animal this is?”

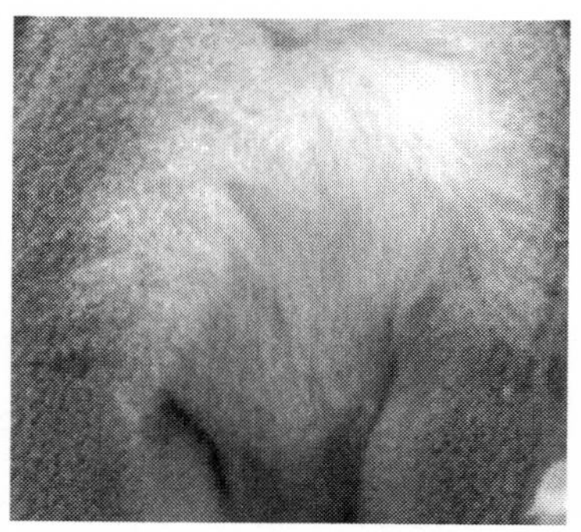

A Baboon? **P310**

Or

A Spider Monkey? **P266**

266

Spider monkey is correct.

"Well done," Maria says. "You got that right. Did you know that all seven species of spider monkeys are under threat and that the black-headed and brown spider monkeys are on the endangered list? It's so sad."

"I read somewhere that spider monkeys are the most intelligent new-world monkeys," you say. "I can't understand why people aren't more careful."

Maria nods. "Spider monkeys make lots of different sounds too. Did you know that they bark like a dog when they are threatened? Now get this one right or back you go."

You are imagining a spider monkey chasing your mailman down the street when Maria pulls another picture out of her pocket.

"Okay, so what do you think this is a picture of?"

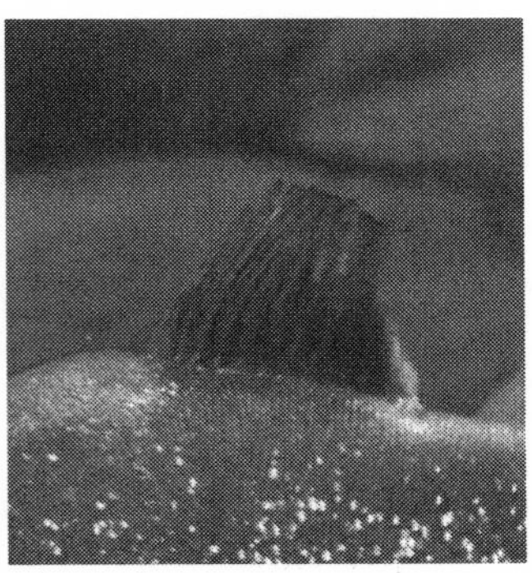

Is it a:

Giant Otter? **P265**

Or

Piranha? **P267**

Piranha is correct.

Rodrigo hands you a guava. "Well done. Have a snack."

"Yes. Well done, smarty pants," Maria says grabbing a guava for herself.

As you bite into the fruit, you suspect Maria is about to tell you more about the well known fish.

"Scientists think there might be as many as 60 different species of piranha," she says. "The locals use their sharp teeth to make weapons."

Rodrigo turns to you. "Did you know that in 2013, on Christmas day, 70 swimmers in Argentina were attacked by piranhas? But attacks are rare," he continues. "So don't worry, normally they just take little fishy nips at you."

Then Maria turns over another photo. "Okay, clever clogs. What's this?"

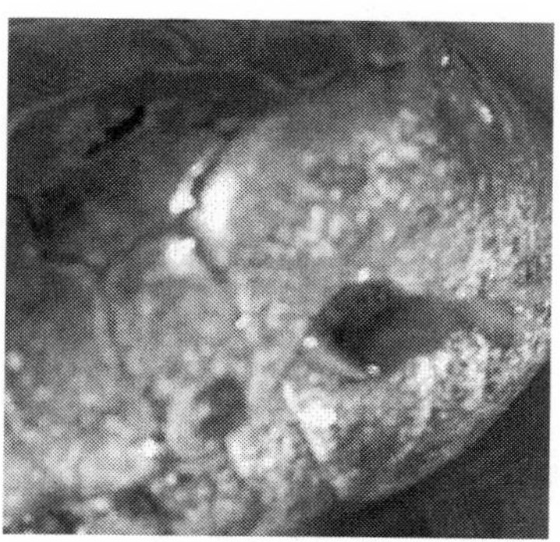

Anaconda? **P268**

Or

Turtle? **P265**

Anaconda is correct.

"Wow!" Maria says. "You're on a roll. I can see I'll have to give you a trickier question next time.

"What? No lecture on anacondas?" you say

"I can if you want me to…"

You hold up a hand. "No that's alright," you say. "I already know it's the biggest snake in the world."

"But did you know that anaconda refers to a group of snakes and that it's the green anaconda that's the biggest?"

Then she flips over another picture. "Okay so what is this?"

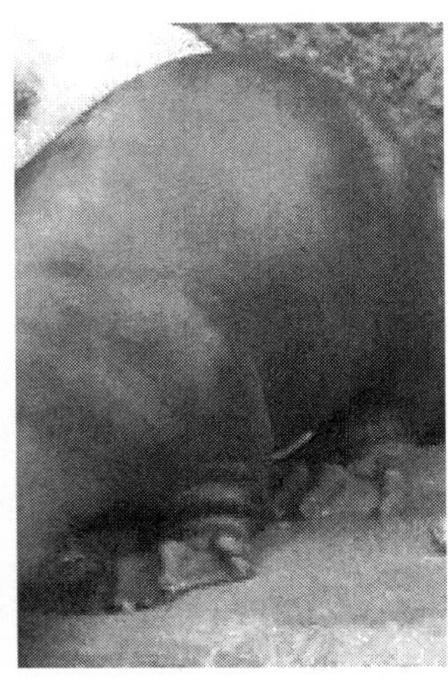

Hippopotamus? **P265**

Or

Giant Otter? **P269**

Giant otter is correct.

"Good guess," Maria says. "You must have seen the webbed feet. Hippos have four toes that aren't webbed, unlike the otter."

You smile. "Yeah and those legs looked a bit short for a hippo. Besides, hippos live in Africa, not South America."

"Very clever. But now it's time to test you on birds," Maria says turning over the next picture. "Over 1500 bird species are found here in the Amazon rainforest. Here's a picture of one you should know."

"You'd better get this one right," Rodrigo says with a wink. "If not, you be going back."

Is it a:

Myna bird? **P295**

Or

Toucan? **P270**

270

Toucan is correct.

"Aren't toucans amazing?" Maria says. "Did you know their beaks come in a variety of colors? Some have yellow or blue or green or black or even a combination of colors."

Rodrigo points at a toucan flying past. "Did you see that?"

You nod. "It's a wonder they can fly with that big beak."

"Their beaks might be long," Maria says. "But they're a lot lighter than people think. They have heaps of tiny air pockets in them to keep the weight down."

You're impressed with Maria's knowledge of birds and wonder which one she'll show you a picture of next.

"Okay, here's one you might remember," she says turning over another picture. "What is this?"

Scarlet Macaw? **P271**
Or
Red Lorikeet? **P303**

Scarlet Macaw is correct.

"Like toucans," Maria says. "Macaws come in all sorts of colors. They're very clever birds too."

As if to illustrate her point, a scarlet macaw comes and sits on a nearby branch. "Hello!" it squawks.

"Hello birdie," you reply.

"Birdie wants a sandwich!"

You look at Maria, then down at the uneaten crust of bread lying on the table. "Is it okay to feed the bird?"

She smiles. "Normally it's not a good idea to feed wild animals, but this is one of the sorcerer's pets so I suppose it's okay."

You toss the crust into the air. The bird flies up, catches it in its beak, and then soars up into the canopy.

"Time for your next picture," Maria says. "I might try something different this time. See if I can fool you and send you back to the start."

"Aw!" you say. "Don't you want me to finish the maze?"

"I do, but I'd like to keep you around for a little while longer. Otherwise the only friend I have is my brother and he's not much fun."

"Hey!" Rodrigo says. "I am too fun!"

"Okay, well you pick a photo then," she says to her brother.

"Right, I will." Rodrigo sorts through the pile, and then turns over a picture. "Okay what is this?"

You study the image. "How am I supposed to tell how

272

big it is from that? Can you give me a hint about how long the animal is?"

"Sure," Rodrigo says. "This one's approximately 14 feet long and it's a reptile."

Is it a:

Anaconda? **P265**

Or a

Caiman? **P273**

Caiman is correct.

"Well done," Rodrigo says. "Caiman are like crocodiles and are one of the most ferocious predators in the Amazon basin. They can grow to over 15 feet in length and weigh more than 800 pounds?"

"I wouldn't want to meet one of those out swimming," you say. "What do they eat?"

Rodrigo laughs. "Anything they can catch! Fish, birds, turtles, small mammals, even people!"

"But," Maria says. "They are also hunted for their skin and meat. So they don't have it all their own way."

"Your clue wasn't much help," you tell Rodrigo. "Anacondas are long and reptiles too."

Rodrigo looks a bit sheepish. "Sorry." Then he turns over another picture. "Here a tough one. What's this?"

Capybara? **P274**

Or

Beaver? **P265**

Capybara is correct.

"Correct," Rodrigo says. "The capybara is the world's largest rodent and a close relative to the guinea pig. They can weigh up to 200 pounds."

"That's a pretty big guinea pig," you say. "Do people eat them?"

"Yup. So do caiman. They're quite social animals and can be found in groups of 100 or more at times."

Then Rodrigo gives Maria a look and raises his eyebrows suspiciously.

She nods.

You wonder what it going on.

"Okay," Rodrigo says. "It's time for your last question. If you get this right you will finish the maze."

"Then you can become a sorcerer's apprentice like us." Maria says. "Won't that be fun!"

"It sure would be nice to learn some of the sorcerer's tricks," you reply. You can just imagine what the kids at school would say when you turn them green, or make spiders appear on their desks.

Rodrigo clears his throat. "Okay here we go. One of these animals isn't found in the Amazon River basin. Can you guess which one?"

Maria holds up her hand. "Be careful. You don't want to end up back at the start now that you're so close."

Rodrigo pulls a bright yellow piece of paper out of his pocket. On it is a list of three animals. He lays it on the table in front of you.

It is time to make a decision. Which of these animals doesn't live in the Amazon River basin?

"Be careful," Maria says. "This could be a trick question."

"Or not," Rodrigo says with a grin on his face.

You read the list. They all seem familiar.

Is it:

Pink Dolphin **P295**

Tarantula **P265**

Or

Leopard **P311**

276

You have chosen to go to sleep.

You lie down, close your eyes and hope for the best. You're pretty sure the sorcerer won't let anything happen to you. After all, why would he provide you with guides if he didn't care about your safety?

Rodrigo and Maria said they'd be back first thing in the morning. Why would they say that if the sorcerer planned to have you eaten during the night? They don't seem the type to tell fibs.

You dream of gigantic spiders and snakes. A couple of times during the night, you get up and throw extra logs on the campfire to keep the wild animals away.

It feels like you've only just dropped off to sleep, when someone starts shaking your arm.

"Wake up sleepyhead!" Maria says. "My brother's cooking breakfast."

You yawn and swing your legs onto the ground. The

smell of eggs makes your stomach rumble.

Rodrigo has dished up three plates, so you sit at the table and prepare to eat.

"Wait," he says. "Before you get breakfast—"

"Let me guess," you interrupt. "I have to answer a question?"

Rodrigo smiles. "You're getting the hang of this maze stuff. At least the first question in the morning is usually an easy one."

"Well I hope so. I'm starving."

Maria comes and sits beside you. "You can do it. Just think logically."

"Okay here we go," says Rodrigo. "If there are three giant otters, and each otter eats three fish per day. How many fish will the three otters eat in a week?"

It is time to make a decision. Is the correct answer:

61 fish? **P279**

Or

63 fish? **P282**

You have chosen tea.

"Oops," says Rodrigo. "Tea is incorrect. Brazil has over 10,000 square miles of coffee plantations. It's China that grows the most tea, followed by India and Kenya."

"Oh well," you say. "What happens now?"

Rodrigo points to a hammock hanging between two trees.

Maria rests her hand lightly on your shoulder. "Looks like you're sleeping in the hammock tonight.

"But what about wild animals?" you ask. "Won't it be dangerous?"

Maria points to the fire and a stack of wood. She walks over and drops a log onto the burning embers. "Not if you keep the fire going."

You're about to ask more questions when Rodrigo and Maria begin to fade. Then they disappear altogether.

"Hey you two! Don't go yet. I still have questions!"

You wait for one of them to reply, but they've gone. So what now? Do you stay up and sit around the campfire all night, or do you try to get some sleep?

It is time to make a decision. Do you:

Go to sleep? **P276**

Or

Sit around the campfire? **P281**

You have chosen 61 Fish.

"Oh no!" Maria says. "If there are three giant otters, and they eat three fish per day each, that's nine fish per day. Nine fish for seven days equals 63 fish."

"Oops," you say. "I never was that good at math."

"Or you could have worked it out by taking one otter that eats 3 fish per day for seven days. That's 21 fish and 3 times 21 is 63." Rodrigo smiles. "Would you like another question so you can move on?"

"Yes please."

Rodrigo pulls another question from the seemingly endless supply in his pocket. "Okay but don't mess this one up or you'll have to go back to the start of the maze."

"What? Right back to the very beginning?"

"Yep," Rodrigo says, giving you a serious look. "Here we go. If you have 29 fish and add 34 fish. How many fish do you have?"

280

Maria taps you on the shoulder. "Remember you can use a calculator if you need to."

"Where would I find a calculator in the jungle?" you ask.

"Use your fingers and toes then," she says. "Just don't get this one wrong."

Rodrigo smiles. "Adding 9 and 4, the last digit of each number, together might give you a hint about which one is right."

It is time to make a decision.

Is 29 fish plus 34 fish:

63 fish? **P282**

Or

61 fish? **P295**

You have chosen to sit around the campfire.

You are alone in the jungle. The fire is a comfort, but it's also too warm to sit very close to the crackling flames. In the light of the fire, you make yourself another sandwich and think.

There are so many sounds. Mainly frogs, from what you can tell. You wonder if any of the frogs you hear croaking are poison dart frogs. You certainly wouldn't want to touch one of those. They secrete enough deadly poison through their skin to stop a person from breathing.

Occasionally you hear something larger moving through the undergrowth. Could it be an anaconda or jaguar? You're near the river too. Do caiman come out of the river to hunt at night?

Maybe the best thing to do would be to go to bed, get some sleep and be ready for morning.

But what if there are dangerous insects like the Brazilian wandering spider about? They're one of the most venomous spiders on earth. And you've read they're nocturnal! Maybe it would be safer to climb up a tree so you are off the ground. You've seen people do that in the movies. But can't spiders climb trees too?

It is time to make a decision. Do you:

Go to sleep? **P276**

Or

Climb up a tree? **P286**

You have chosen 63 fish.

"Well done," Maria says. 63 fish is correct. Let's eat!"

You tuck in to your breakfast. The toast is crispy and the eggs are done just how you like them. "You're not a bad cook, Rodrigo. Is there any more toast?"

Rodrigo hands you another slice, and then passes you a jar of lime marmalade. "Try this, it's great."

Maria looks over at you. "Brazil produces over 700,000 tons of lime each year."

You spread a thick layer of the sticky, green jelly onto your toast and take a bite. "Didn't the old sailors eat citrus fruit to stop scurvy?"

Rodrigo nods. "Lemons and limes use to be carried on sailing ships. Limes originated in Asia, but now they're grown all around the world."

"This tastes better than grape," you say, after another bite. "But then I'm so hungry almost anything would taste good."

Maria gives you a funny look. "Anything?"

Oh no. Why is she looking at you like that? Has she got some new test in mind?

As you are about to take another bite, there is a puff of smoke and you find yourself holding a sandwich.

"Wow where did that come from?"

"The sorcerer!" Rodrigo and Maria say in unison.

"What's it made of?" you ask.

"Queijo," says Rodrigo.

"But what does that mean in English?"

Then you realize you've been trapped. They are going to ask you a question.

Both Rodrigo and Maria are giggling.

"So what do you think a queijo sandwich is made of?" asks Maria. "If you get the answer right you get to come with us further through the maze."

"And if I get it wrong?"

Maria grins. "You get a big surprise!"

It is time to make a decision. What is queijo?

Is it:

Cheese? **P288**

Chicken? **P256**

Or

Should you take a chance and go to **P303**?

You have chosen 32.

"Well done," says Rodrigo, appearing out of nowhere.

Your eyes go wide. "What are you doing here?"

"It's nearly morning," he says.

"I'm pleased to hear that. It's creepy out here in the dark."

"While I was away I learned a new trick," he says. "It's fun being a sorcerer's apprentice." Rodrigo snaps his fingers and Maria appears.

You step back in surprise. "Wow that's a good trick! Can you teach me?"

"Maybe, but you'll have to become a sorcerer's apprentice first."

"I've been learning tricks too," says Maria. She walks over to the camp kitchen and snaps her fingers. In a puff of green smoke, the table is set and a dozen eggs and bread for toast appears. Maria grins at you. "Seeing I've done the shopping, you two get to make the breakfast."

You snap your finger a couple of times in the hope that some of Maria's magic has worn off on you. But the eggs sit in their carton, uncooked.

Rodrigo looks amused at your feeble attempt. "Poached or fried?"

"Is this a trick question?" you ask. "I don't want to end up back at the beginning of the maze."

Rodrigo shakes his head. "Don't worry, it's not a trick."

You're relieved to hear it. "Fried please."

In a flash, three plates are loaded with golden-brown toast and steaming eggs.

"Hey, why are my eggs flecked with green?" you ask.

Rodrigo smiles. "I like green eggs, don't you?"

You take a small bite. "Yum, parsley."

"It's my own special recipe," Rodrigo says.

You're hungry, so you shovel a forkful of food into your mouth.

"Wait till you try my chocolate popcorn."

You nearly choke on your food. "Chocolate popcorn? Are you serious?"

"Not really. I was just trying to lead into the next question. If you get it right you get to move on to the next part of the maze."

You eat fast, worried that you'll be sent off somewhere before you finish. Around these two, you never know when you'll get your next meal. When the last of your eggs are gone, you turn to Rodrigo and smile. "What happens if I get the question wrong?"

"You might find yourself up a tree," he says with a grin. "Now listen carefully. Cocoa beans are the dried and partially fermented seeds of the cacao tree. That's what chocolate is made from. But where did the cacao tree originate?"

South America? **P296**

Or

West Africa? **P299**

286

You have decided to climb up a tree.

You decide to climb a big tree next to the camp. You grab a piece of rope and a bottle of water and start up. Once you work your way up to the first major branch, the branches are evenly spaced and the climbing gets easier.

Some of the branches are covered in moss, lichens and other tiny plants. There's a whole jungle growing up here. Sometimes there are so many vines and plants it makes getting a grip difficult.

Your head snaps upward when you hear movement in the branches above you. What could it be?

You nearly fall out of the tree when a pair of large yellow eyes stare back at you. Despite the warm sticky air all around you, a shiver runs down your back. Maybe if you don't move whatever it is won't attack.

You freeze, and stare back. The eyes seem oddly familiar somehow.

Then you hear purring. Do jaguars purr? Surely not.

"Meowww!" comes the call from up the tree. The eyes move closer.

You are about to climb back down when there is a rustle of leaves and the cat jump onto the branch beside you and starts rubbing itself against your leg.

"Meowww!"

"What are you doing in the jungle kitty?" you say, scratching the purring cat under its chin. "Are you the sorcerer's cat?"

"Meowww!"

As the cat moves against your hand, greedy for more petting, you notice a collar around its neck. Attached to the collar is a piece of paper.

"I bet I know what this is puss," you say as you remove the paper and turn on your flashlight. "This will be another one of those confounded question."

"Me—owww!"

The writing is small, but you can just make out the words.

It says:

WHAT ARE YOU DOING UP THE TREE? GO TO BED OR I'LL SEND YOU BACK TO THE BEGINNING OF THE MAZE.

The note is signed, The Sorcerer.

What do you do?

Climb down and go to sleep? **P276**

Or

Take a chance and turn to **P295**

You have chosen cheese.

"Well done," Maria says. "Eat your cheese sandwich and then let's go. We've still got quite a lot of ground to cover before we reach the end of the maze."

You stuff the sandwich in your mouth. It could be ages before you get to eat again if you get trapped in the maze somewhere. Better safe than sorry.

Rodrigo and Maria get ready to move on. They are stuffing equipment into packs.

"Aren't we taking the boat?" you ask.

Rodrigo shakes his head. "No the next section is a canopy walk up in the treetops."

You look up at the towering trees all around you. A rope ladder hangs down from one of them. "Are we going to climb up that?" you say pointing towards the ladder.

"Good guess," says Rodrigo. "The sorcerer has made a special walkway so we can discover the variety of wildlife that lives high above the forest floor."

Maria looks up from her packing. "You're not afraid of heights are you?"

You swallow. "It depends."

Maria snaps her fingers and you float up into the air about three feet. "I've been learning a few tricks. If you fall, just yell out my name and I'll snap my fingers. That will stop you from falling."

You feel a little better after seeing Maria's powerful magic. Being a sorcerer's apprentice certainly has its advantages.

After filling water bottles and putting pieces of fruit in your daypacks, the three of you head off towards the rope ladder.

As you near the tree, you look up and spot a narrow bridge running from the tree's upper branches to another platform, on a giant tree about 100 yards away.

"Is that where we're going? It sure is a long way up." you say.

"Don't worry," Rodrigo says. "As long as you follow us and do what we say, you'll be fine."

Like acrobats, Rodrigo and Maria scamper up the rope ladder. Higher and higher they climb.

A parrot flits down from an upper branch and lands on a shrub nearby. "Better get a move on!" it squawks.

You tighten the straps on your pack and start up the ladder. The rope sways a bit as you climb, but before long you are standing next to Maria and Rodrigo high up in the crook of the tree. The swing bridge swoops out over the canopy of the smaller trees below.

"Follow me," Rodrigo says as he steps out onto the bridge.

Maria follows her brother, and then you bring up the rear. The bridge is wobbly, but you soon get used to the movement and time your step to counter the swing.

When you look down, you get a bird's eye view of the jungle. "Wow, this sure gives a different perspective of the rainforest," you say.

Birds fly below you over a carpet of green tree tops. In the distance, the Amazon River winds its way into a vast expanse of jungle that stretches as far as the eye can see. On one of the trees below, a family of monkeys sit eating plantains.

When you reach the far platform, Rodrigo and Maria are waiting for you with silly grins on their faces.

"What are you grinning at?" you ask.

Rodrigo reaches for his pocket

"Really? I have to answer questions way up here?"

Rodrigo shrugs. "No. You don't have to. You can do the canopy walk by yourself if you like."

Without waiting for an answer, he reaches for a vine. "Good luck." Then he swings off into the jungle.

Maria grabs a vine. "Oh, and watch out for snakes, they love it up here in the trees." Then she swings off after her brother.

"Snakes? Stop! Wait for me!" you cry out, looking for another vine to swing on. But there are none. You look around the platform. All you see is another bridge leading to a tree further along.

What do you do? Do you:

Go back the way you came? **P291**

Or

Carry on across the next swing bridge? **P292**

You have chosen to go back the way you came.

You start back the way you came. If you go back to the rope ladder, you can climb down and walk the short distance to camp. Once there, you can wait for Rodrigo and Maria to turn up. Surely they won't abandon you in the jungle. After all, isn't it their job to make sure you get through the maze?

But as you step out on the swing bridge to retrace your steps, the bridge is at a funny angle. You peer towards the other end and see why. A large snake has wrapped itself around the handrail and is twisting the bridge to one side. The weird angle doesn't seem to be worrying the snake. It has looped itself around the handrail and is slithering along towards you.

There is a sturdy looking branch just below you. Maybe you should climb down onto that to escape the snake. You might just reach it if you climb over the handrail and hang down. Or should you go across the second bridge and see where it leads?

Whatever you do, it needs to be fast, because the snake has seen you and is slithering your way.

It is time for a quick decision. Do you:

Go across the next bridge? **P292**

Or

Climb down onto the tree branch? **P293**

292

You have decided to cross the next bridge.

This second bridge is a bit wobblier than the first, but at least you're heading away from that big hungry-looking snake. A parrot lands on the rope railing.

"Hello birdie," you say.

The parrot twists its head sideways and eyeballs you. "Hello birdie!"

"So what now?" you ask the bird.

"How should I know? I'm a parrot!"

"But you just answered me! You're not a normal parrot."

"Snake! Snake! Better get a move on!" the parrot squawks.

You look over your shoulder. The snake is crossing the second bridge after you.

You look around for somewhere to go, but there isn't another bridge to cross. Pinned on the trunk is a sign. It says:

PICK A VINE OR YOU'LL BE LUNCH
ONE KNOT OR TWO? WHAT'S YOUR HUNCH?

Wrapped around the tree trunk are two vines. One has a single knot tied in its end, the other has two knots. You hear a hiss. The snake is close. Which vine do you pick?

(Hint: how many stars are on the Chilean flag?)

Swing on the vine with one knot **P304**

Or

Swing on the vine with two knots. **P303**

You have decided to climb down onto the tree branch.

You climb over the rope railing and get ready to drop down onto the branch below. But out here on the edge of the bridge, everything seems much higher. The bridge sways slightly in the breeze. You feel light-headed and your knees tremble. "Help!"

"Hold my hand!"

It's Maria. She's standing beside you.

"On three, jump with me. Don't worry, I won't let you fall." Maria lets go of the bridge and snaps her fingers.

You

are

F

A

L

L

I

N

G

There is a flash of light, a puff of smoke, and then nothing. The next thing you know, you are sitting on the ground and your dizziness is starting to fade.

"That was a close call," Maria says. "And all because you made a silly choice. I have to give you a really hard question now as punishment. If you get it wrong you'll go back to the very beginning of the maze."

"And if I get it right?"

294

Maria has a serious expression on her face. "You'll see."

She reaches into a pocket and pulls out a piece of paper. The paper is red and there is a big question mark at the top. "Okay here we go. Think carefully now."

"The Pantanal is a huge wetland in the Amazon basin that is sanctuary to migrating bird species, a breeding ground for hundreds of fish species and home to hundreds of mammals and reptiles. Which of these five choices is the biggest threats to the Pantanal?"

Is it:

Cattle ranching? **P298**

Poaching? **P303**

Commercial Fishing? **P298**

Mining? **P295**

All of the above **P304**

Welcome back to Camp 1

"Welcome back to Camp 1. You got that last question wrong didn't you?" Maria smiles and walks towards an ice chest sitting under the table. "Like another cold soda? You must be thirsty with all this zipping around."

Rodrigo laughs. "The sorcerer is a tough taskmaster isn't he?"

Maria and Rodrigo grab a soda each and the three of you sit down at the picnic table.

"So what now?" you ask.

Rodrigo reaches for his pocket. "You'll have to answer the questions again. At least they'll be easier this time."

"Assuming you've been paying attention," Maria says.

Spreading the paper out on the table in front of him, Rodrigo starts reading. "Okay, here we go again. Brazil is the world's largest producer of what common product. Is it:"

Coffee? **P260**

Or is it

Tea? **P278**

You have chosen South America.

"Good pick," Rodrigo says. "Even though most of the world's cacao is grown in West Africa these days, the cacao plant originated in the Amazon basin of South America."

"So do I win a prize?" you ask.

Maria giggles. "No, but you do get to ride with us in the boat again. We're going hunting for electric eels."

"Really? There are eels that run on electricity here in the Amazon?"

Maria laughs. "They don't actually light up, but they sure can give you a jolt. Some generate over 600 volts. Imagine sticking your finger in an electrical socket, only worse."

"Shocking!"

Maria smiles at your pun. "But they're not really eels, even though they look like one," she says. "They're actually a type of knife fish, which is a cousin of the catfish. They use their electricity for hunting and defense."

Rodrigo chuckles. "Did you know there's an electric eel in Tennessee that has its own twitter account? It automatically sends out a message whenever it lets off an electric charge?"

Your forehead creases and you shake your head. "Do I look that gullible?"

"I'm telling you the truth," Rodrigo says. "The Japanese have also used an electric eel to light up a Christmas tree. Google it."

"I will," you say. "I like learning new things about animals."

Rodrigo raises his eyebrows a couple of times. "Hmmm. Do you just?" He glances over at his sister.

Maria smiles and nods to her brother.

They are up to something and you're not sure you like the looks they're giving each other. "Okay you two, what's going on?"

Rodrigo pulls a piece of paper out of his pocket. "It just so happens the sorcerer has prepared an animal riddle for you. I'm looking forward to seeing how you do with this one. It's a bit tricky."

He holds the paper up and reads:

I MIGHT BE BLUE
OR I MIGHT BE RED
SOMETIMES I'M BLACK
WITH A YELLOW HEAD
YOU'D BETTER WATCH OUT
AND HEAR WHAT I'VE SAID
BECAUSE IF YOU TOUCH ME
YOU COULD END UP DEAD

Rodrigo looks over at you. "So what am I?"

A snake? **P301**

A frog? **P304**

Or

A spider? **P303**

298

Have another go.

You are partially correct, but there are many threats to the Pantanal. Would you like to try that last question again?

Yes **P294**

Or

No. Take me to the correct answer. **P304**

You have chosen West Africa.

Rodrigo looks at you and shakes his head. "That was a good guess because most of the world's cacao is grown in West Africa these days, followed by Indonesia. But, unfortunately for you, it originated in the Amazon basin of South America."

Rodrigo raises his hand.

You can tell he's about to snap his fingers and send you off somewhere. "Wait—"

POOF!

You are high up a tree on a rickety platform built of branches. What are you meant to do now?

Then you see a small sign attached to a branch. It says:

CHOOSE THE RIGHT VINE AND YOU'LL SWING BACK DOWN
BUT IF YOU CHOOSE WRONG, YOU'LL HAVE A FROWN.

When you look around, you see three vines twisted around the trunk of the tree. One has a single knot tied in its end. Another has two knots, and the third has three knots. But which one do you pick? And what happens if you choose wrong, will you fall to the ground and hurt yourself?

You're studying the vines trying to make a decision when you hear a growl from below. It's a jaguar, and it's climbing up the tree towards you!

A parrot lands on a branch beside you. "Jaguar! Jaguar! Better get moving!"

Quick it's time to choose a vine and swing away before

300

the jaguar get you!

Which of the three vines do you choose?

(Hint: how many stripes are on the Bolivian flag?)

One knot? **P256**

Two knots? **P303**

Or

Three knots? **P304**

Oops, that's not right.

"The correct answer is frog," Rodrigo says. "The poison dart frog, to be exact. There are over 100 different species of poisonous frogs in the Amazon basin. The natives sometimes use frog poison to dip their arrows in."

"Ouch," you say. "I thought they used curare?"

"They do, but frog poison works too." Then he gives you a sad look. "Unfortunately, because you got the wrong answer, I have to send you off into the jungle again."

He clicks his fingers.

In a flash, you are high up a tree, standing on a small platform built out of branches about as big around as your arm. What are you meant to do now?

Then you see a small sign. It says:

CHOOSE A VINE AND SWING BACK DOWN
BUT IF YOU CHOOSE WRONG, YOU'LL HAVE A FROWN.

When you look around you see three vines twisted around the trunk of the tree. One has a single knot tied in its end, another has two knots and the third has three. But which one do you pick? And what happens if you choose wrong?

You are studying the vines when you hear a hiss below you. It is a huge green anaconda! And it's slithering up the tree towards you. Its tongue flicks in and out of its mouth, tasting your scent.

A parrot lands on a branch beside you. "Snake! Snake! Better get moving!"

302

Quick- it's time to choose a vine and swing off before the anaconda gets you!

Which of the three vines to you choose?

(Hint: how many colors are there on the Columbian flag?)

One knot? **P256**

Two knots? **P303**

Or

Three knots? **P304**

Welcome back to Camp 1

"Welcome back to Camp 1. You got that last question wrong didn't you?" Maria smiles and walks towards an ice chest sitting under the table. "Like another cold soda? You must be thirsty with all this zipping around."

Rodrigo laughs. "That sorcerer is a tough taskmaster isn't he?"

Maria and Rodrigo grab a soda each and the three of you sit down at the picnic table.

"So what now?" you ask.

Rodrigo reaches for his pocket. "You'll have to answer the questions again. At least they'll be easier this time."

"Assuming you've been paying attention," Maria says.

Spreading the paper out on the table in front of him, Rodrigo starts reading. "Okay, here we go again. Brazil is the world's largest producer of what common product. Is it:"

Coffee? **P260**

Or is it

Tea? **P278**

Congratulations you have reached the final stage of the maze.

"Hooray! You got that right," Rodrigo and Maria say in unison.

"Phew!" you say. "So, what now? More questions?"

Maria rests her hand on your shoulder. "Now you just have one more part of the maze to get through and you can become a sorcerer's apprentice, just like us!"

You give Maria and Rodrigo a smile. "Okay let's do it!"

Maria leads you to a table set up in a clearing and brings out a number of photographs. "All you have to do now it identify these animals."

"I'm pretty good at animals," you say. "Ah but these aren't normal photos," Rodrigo says. "They've been specially made by the sorcerer. And you know how tricky he can get."

Maybe you've spoken too soon. "Tricky how?"

Maria giggles. "You'll see."

She lays a picture face up on the table. "What animal is this?"

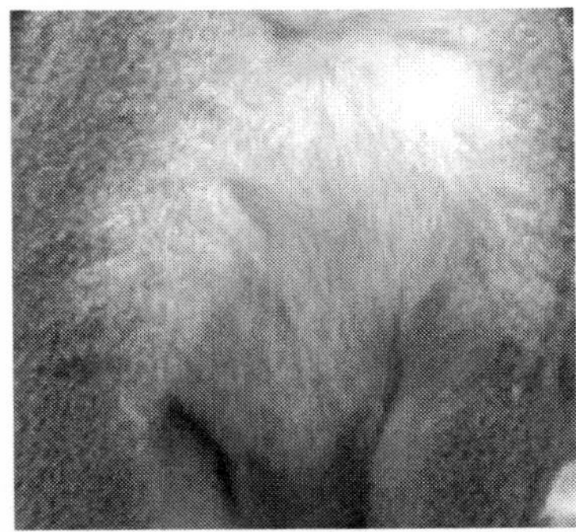

"Hey! Aren't you going to show me all of it! That could be anything!"

Maria shrugs. "I did warn you. The sorcerer never makes it too easy to become an apprentice."

"And," Rodrigo says. "If you get one wrong, you have to go back to the start of this section."

It is time to make a decision. It the picture above a picture of:

A Baboon? **P265**

or

A Spider Monkey? **P266**

List of Choices

Oops, you've been sent back to the beginning of the maze!

How did you get here? You're back at the jungle clearing.

On the river bank, Maria and Rodrigo stand beside their small boat with the outboard motor attached to its stern and the blue roof to protect its occupants from the hot tropical sun.

Rodrigo waves, "Hello again."

Maria walks towards you. "So, here we are, back at the beginning." she says. "You must have made a really big mistake. Don't worry, my brother and I know the Amazon well, we'll help you through."

"But, as you know, before we go upriver," Rodrigo says, pulling a piece of paper out of his pocket, "the sorcerer wants me to ask you a question. If you get it right, we can leave. At least the answers should be easier to get right this time. Assuming you were paying attention.

"Here goes. How many different species of fish are known to live in the Amazon River?"

It is time to make a choice. Which do you choose?

The Amazon River has over 3000 species of fish. **P214**

Or

The Amazon River has less that 1000 species of fish. **P217**

Congratulations! You made it!

You are suddenly transported up into a massive tree house high in the canopy. It is like nothing you've ever seen. Shelves of books tower to the sky. High above, mighty condors soar amongst the clouds.

In the middle of the room, a boy about your age sits behind a large desk. He is dressed in colorful robes and has a pointy cap on. A jumble of books are open on the desk in front of him.

"So you finally made it," he says.

You nod and then look around. "Are you the sorcerer?"

"Yep!" The boy snaps his fingers. "Abracadabra!" In a puff of pink smoke, a colorful macaw appears on his arm.

The bird tilts its head and stares at you. "Hello birdie!" the macaw squawks. "Took you long enough!"

The sorcerer snaps his fingers again and a comfortable

chair appears. "Take a seat and I'll explain."

The chair is huge and soft, like sitting in a cloud. Then he snaps his fingers again and Rodrigo and Maria appear.

Maria smiles at you and giggles. "This is where the sorcerer makes up all the questions for his mazes. Isn't it a wonderful place?"

You can't help but agree. Never have you seen bookshelves so high. When you look out the window, the jungle stretches for miles in every direction.

The sorcerer gives you a serious glare as he leans forward. "I have so many mazes to make I'm having to do 100 jobs at once. I was hoping you might like to become an apprentice." He snaps his fingers and a cute little spider monkey lands on your lap. "There are lots of benefits you know and to tell you the truth, I could really do with some help."

As you give the monkey a scratch, it wraps long arms around you and gives you a cuddle.

You must admit you're interested. Going through the maze was a lot of fun and becoming one of the sorcerer's apprentices would be exciting. "What would I have to do?"

"You'd help make up the questions for my maze. And every now and then, you get to act as guide for someone new. Like Maria and Rodrigo did for you."

"I can think of lots of cool questions," you say. "Did you know that Pluto is 3,670,050,000 miles from the sun?"

"Hmm… interesting," he says. "You sound like a natural. Maybe you'd like to help me make a maze in space, or one about time travel, or an unusual road trip?" The sorcerer stands up. "You don't have to make your mind up right now."

You give the spider monkey another pat as it picks through your hair looking for fleas.

"I'd better get back to work," the sorcerer says. "I've a million interesting facts to look up."

And with that, the sorcerer disappears in a puff of smoke.

The next thing you know you are back at home, smarter than you were when you left and thinking of all sorts of interesting questions and riddles you'll make up if you decide to become the sorcerer's apprentice.

THE END

Why not check out the List of Choice on **P306** for sections of the story you might have missed.

Or

You could help the sorcerer by logging on to Amazon.com leaving a short review for this book.

314

More You Say Which Way Adventures

(Available from Amazon.com)

Between The Stars
Pirate Island
Mystic Portal
Dungeon of Doom
Stranded Starship
Dinosaur Canyon
Island of Giants
Creepy House
Lost in Lion Country
Once Upon an Island
In the Magician's House
Secrets of Glass Mountain
Danger on Dolphin Island
Volcano of Fire
Dragons Realm
Deadline Delivery
The Sorcerer's Maze Adventure Quiz (book 1)
The Sorcerer's Maze Time Machine (book 2)

316

YouSayWhichWay.com

318

Made in the USA
Coppell, TX
28 November 2020